The Balloon Lady
and Other People I Know

Emerging Writers in Creative Nonfiction

The Balloon Lady and Other People I Know

Jeanne Marie Laskas

DUQUESNE UNIVERSITY PRESS
PITTSBURGH, PENNSYLVANIA

This book is published by Duquesne University Press
600 Forbes Avenue
Pittsburgh, PA 15282–0101

Copyright © 1996 by Duquesne University Press

Library of Congress Cataloging-in-Publication Data

Laskas, Jeanne Marie, 1958–
    The balloon lady and other people I know / by Jeanne Marie Laskas.
        p.   cm.
    ISBN 0–8207–0271–4 (cloth). — ISBN 0–8207–0266–8 (paper)
    I. Title
AC8.L36   1996
081—dc20   95–50215
                                                                                    CIP

Credits

"A Vacuum Cleaner Salesman" originally appeared as "Nature Abhors a Vacuum Cleaner Salesman" in *The Washington Post Magazine*, May 29, 1988. "Magic" originally appeared in *Creative Nonfiction*, No. 3, 1995. "The Balloon Lady" originally appeared as "The Dotty Duchess of the Wild Blue Yonder" in *The Philadelphia Inquirer Magazine*, September 6, 1987. "Pinball" originally appeared as "Pinball is Back" in *Life*, September 1990. "The Slinky Lady" originally appeared as "This Immortal Coil" in *The Philadelphia Inquirer Magazine*, July 11, 1993. "The Pet Shrink" originally appeared in *The Washington Post Magazine*, November 20, 1988. "A Groundhog" originally appeared as "Rodent Love" in *The Washington Post Magazine*, June 5, 1994. "Bargemen of the Monongahela" originally appeared in *Pittsburgh Magazine*, November, 1984. "The Pig Man" originally appeared as "Living High on the Hog" in *The Washington Post Magazine*, May 28, 1989. "What's Lithuanian?" originally appeared in *The Washington Post Magazine*, July 8, 1990. "Branson in My Rearview Mirror" originally appeared in *GQ*, May, 1994. "Cats" originally appeared in *The Washington Post Magazine*, February 28, 1993. "Tom Cruise" originally appeared as "What's Driving Tom Cruise?" in *Life*, June, 1990. "Geraldo" originally appeared as "Has Love Changed Geraldo?" in *Woman's Day*, February 5, 1991. "Our Barbies, Our Selves" originally appeared in *The Philadelphia Inquirer Magazine*, March 5, 1989. "A Garden in Winter" originally appeared in *The Washington Post Magazine*, December 13, 1992.

Design by Jennifer Matesa

This book is printed on acid-free paper.

For my mother, the original balloon lady.

Contents

Acknowledgments

For me, this book is a look back in time. All of these stories were written over the past ten or so years, and published as magazine articles. They are about people I'd just met, as well as people I've known all my life. They represent not only my experiences, but events shared with friends, family and editors who provided ideas and guidance.

I'd like to say thank you to a few of these people.

First, to Alex Levy, for his love, support and for the countless insights he brought to the pages of this book and continues to bring to the chapters of my life. Also, to my mother, for whom this book is dedicated, and my father, for his example of integrity. To my sister, Kristin, for her guidance and encouragement. To my brother, John, for showing me the meaning of the word "enthusiasm," and to his wife, Eileen, for laughing with me and not giving up until her name was in print. To Alyson, John, Joe and Tom Laskas, Katie Martin, and Peter and Matthew Caltabiano for keeping the child in me alive. To Hugh Martin, for keeping me laughing and taking me shopping, and to James Caltabiano for humoring my sister, Claire, as she remains dedicated to her status as my most devoted audience. Thank you, Claire.

I'd like to say a special thank you to Lee Gutkind, editor of the *Emerging Writers in Creative Nonfiction* series, for standing beside me—and in front of me—and making this book possible. And to Susan Wadsworth-Booth and the editors at Duquesne for their patience and hard work. Also, to the generous members of the proofreading committee: AAL, Barbara Klein, John Laskas and Amy Levy.

There are numerous editors I'd like to thank who have helped me along the way, most notably Bruce Vanwyngarden, formerly of *Pittsburgh Magazine,* Jay Lovinger and Steve Petranek at *Life,* Bob Thompson and Linton Weeks at *The Washington Post,* Art Carey and Avery Rome at *The Philadelphia Inquirer* and David Granger at *GQ.*

Thank you, too, to so many of my friends for enriching me: Marie McCormick, Kit Ayars, Nancy Mosser, BK, Beth Marcello, Ellen Perlmutter, Bruce Dobler, Vince Rause, Lynn Cullen, Sally Wiggin, and Fred and Joanne Rogers.

Finally, and perhaps most importantly, I'd like to thank all of the people featured in this book who abided my tape recorder and notepad, and allowed me the privilege of stepping into their lives.

—jml

Introduction

Two of the essays in this book are about an old lady I used to know. She died a few years ago, at 89. I think a lot about her. So much of what I write involves experiences lived in the spirit of Constance Wolf.

She was an adventurer. For no particular reason, she made it her life's work to fly balloons. She became the first woman and the first American to pilot a gas balloon over the Swiss Alps and, in 1961, floated for 40 miserable hours over Texas and Oklahoma, coming down with world records for endurance, altitude, distance and 12 other titles. She campaigned for, and with, U.S. presidents in balloons. She once gave a balloon, "La Coquette," to Mike Todd for his movie, *Around the World in Eighty Days*, and then flew with him in it a few times over Paris and London, promoting the film and throwing candy down to children.

For no particular reason. There was no master plan, there were no goals. She was not intent on becoming anything. She lived adventure by adventure, each scheme coming into her head quite unexpectedly and sporadically and urgently.

I became enchanted by Mrs. Wolf when I first met her over a decade ago. I was drawn by her stories and the freedom they represented, by her love of the absurd, by her way of throwing not only caution, but also reason and meaning, to the wind. Day after day I would sit with her in her parlor, sipping sherry, rolling over with laughter as she sat in her triangular-shaped chair, allowing these extraordinary tales to unfold with the most hypnotic rhythm: bang, joke, bang, bang, joke. I felt so privileged that she would choose to put on this show for me.

Sometimes now I wonder—who is the more privileged, the listener or the storyteller?

Not until more recently, not until I sat with Mrs. Wolf in a nursing home after she had been robbed by a stroke of her speech, did it occur to me what it must have meant for her to have someone to tell her stories to. I would watch the nurses come in to change her sheets, or to stick things in her, or to force her to take pills that she would hide under her tongue as if to avenge the gods for this degrading fate. I would say to the nurses: "You know, she's a world famous balloonist!" They would look at me. How could I make them understand? I wanted them to see that this lady was different from the lady in 301 with the feeding tube, the one down the hall hollering through the night, and all of the others.

The nurses would nod, smile politely, and move on.

What if you lived adventures with no one taking notice, no one to experience your experiences? Would all the adventures just disappear? Would the adventures have happened at all?

Recording adventures became a way for me to think about writing. Somewhere inside I must have had the thought: What if I were the 80-year-old woman and there was no 25-year-old to sit in my parlor, sip sherry and laugh at the ridiculous things I did? And

I wanted to do ridiculous things—undoubtedly in the spirit of Mrs. Wolf. I wanted to go off for no particular reason and travel as deeply as I could into something that didn't matter, not really, not until you took it home and thought about it. Then it would begin mattering deeply.

Life with a vacuum cleaner salesman, life on a barge, life as a gypsy, life in a pinball factory, life as a magician. I began exploring the everydayness of everyday worlds. I like searching for the extraordinary in the ordinary. Often I am caught offguard by what I find there. For instance—madness. Every once in a while I will be surprised by madness: the madness of a dog trainer, the madness haunting a midwestern town, the madness tiptoeing on the edges of my own psyche. My purpose is to go into these worlds without purpose, my mind as blank a canvas as I can scrub clean. The mind! The mind, I've concluded, is overrated. The meaning your mind makes is nothing compared to the meaning your skin can find. Reporting, to me, starts with the skin. You can feel when something important is happening long before your intellect catches on.

"What was that about?" I'll ask myself when I finally return home and attempt to understand an experience in terms of how it leaves me feeling. Am I a nervous wreck? Then perhaps the person I've just spent time with was more troubled than I am aware of. Am I angry? Then perhaps I've just been duped. Am I so moved by some act of tenderness that I can't hold back tears?

I ask these questions and have these conversations, on paper, as I begin to record my notes. It's only through writing and feeling, and feeling and writing, that I am able to discover the truth an experience holds for me.

Recently someone asked me why I'm always writing about such odd places and people and things. Well, the word he used was "weird." Weird? Not really. I write about places and people and things because that's what there is to write about. And I let them affect me. And it is in that process—if I am paying attention and if I am lucky—that I might discover what is generally hidden: the unusual, the painful, the shameful, the holy.

How was I to know that when the dog trainer was a boy he was attacked by a giant, evil poodle in his dreams? How was I to know that the vacuum cleaner's father was a failed Fuller Brush man? How was I to know Geraldo Rivera drives a boat, "Bubba," to work? How was I to know, when I first met Mrs. Wolf, that so many adventures would be hidden inside this old lady sitting on a farm tractor, dressed in army fatigues and pearls, with a thin, black veil stretched across her face?

"Weird," people used to say about Mrs. Wolf's outfits, and certainly her veil. I learned to ignore the veil—and, later, the camouflage and the makeup and the other things people use, believing themselves to appear more beautiful or, at least, less ugly. My interest is in finding the hidden truths that make the camouflage necessary or, at least, understandable.

I'm not sure how I pick a particular place or person or thing to write about. Who knows why a person is drawn in one direction rather than another? I believe the wind has a lot to do with it. Some people choose to fight the wind, or hide from it, or tumble in its push and pull. Others ride it, as in a balloon. I believe that what you write about and how you write, what you create and how you create, is up to your relationship with this wind, or this muse, or this God, or whatever it is that carries you into a chance meeting with an old lady you couldn't, and can't, forget.

A Vacuum Cleaner Salesman

1

"Jiminy Cricket!" Steve Sklar will shout, trying to impress the lady of the house with a truly disgusting ball of dirt he has just sucked from her cleanest looking carpet. "Holy Toledo!" he will say, displaying the dirt ball just so on the coffee table, on a perfectly white cloth, proving that dirt is everywhere, that cleanliness is an illusion. For 15 years, Steve Sklar has supported a wife and three lovely children on that certain truth.

He is a vacuum cleaner salesman—a door-to-door Electrolux salesman, to be specific. He is a survivor. Selling vacuum cleaners isn't a field people go into anymore. Even Sklar calls it a dying art. In Washington D.C., there are but two door-to-door Electrolux salesmen left, counting Sklar. Nevertheless, he pulls in $75,000 in an average year. In a better-than-average year—two years ago—Sklar sold a whopping 407 machines, ranking him 16th among some 15,000 Electrolux salesmen nationwide.

He is the son of a Fuller Brush man, so you could say that the art of selling is in his blood. It is a hard thing for him to put into words, explaining why he's so good at selling vacuum cleaners door-to-door. "The whole key to direct selling is that you have to live, breathe and sweat the stuff," he says.

It is not unusual for him to make sweeping statements about the vacuum cleaner business: "There's a certain philosophicalness to my being." He says, "Lately, I've thought there has got to be more to this life than just selling a vacuum cleaner." He says, "Diversification takes the place of single purposefulness of mind." He says, "Maybe that's what's called success. You don't think of anything else but making money and selling, whatever you're selling. God help you if you think back. You say, 'Where did my whole daggone life go?'"

Sklar is 46 years old, and, to glance at him, coming up your front walk, toward your front door, a stranger in a simulated leather jacket with "Electrolux" written across the breast and pencil-holder loops sewn onto the sleeve, you could say here is a middle-aged man just like any other middle-aged man; here is a man coming to the end of one season, headed into another. Here is a man who pursued the American dream and got it, doing what his father did, only doing it better. Here is a man who earned tons of money, not to mention bonuses like free TVs and VCRs and radios and jewels and vacations to faraway lands. Here is a man who worked his brains out making a good living and raising a decent family. Here is another accomplished middle-aged man standing at the threshold, saying, "Now what?"

He rings the bell. He doesn't pause. He opens the storm door and knocks. He doesn't pause. He slips his business card into an available crack, then heads next door. He doesn't use driveways, paths. He tramples right over the lawn, to the next house, where he rings the bell, opens the storm door, knocks, slips the card into the crack and, every five houses or so, takes out a sugarless candy and sucks on it. There is a certain rhythm to this.

His van is parked a few blocks away and it is filled with Electrolux vacuum cleaners, all of them in boxes, waiting to be born.

The vacuum cleaner Sklar is peddling goes for $699. Add the shampooer/floor polisher onto that, and the whole package comes to a little over $1,100. "This is the Mercedes of vacuum cleaners," he will tell you, which is why he sells in neighborhoods where people drive Mercedes-Benzes. The target area this day is a swank set of avenues in northwest Washington.

And so he rings doorbell after doorbell, and one after another the doors open, and one after another the doors close. It goes on like this for three hours, but Sklar shows no signs of giving up. He will leave no doorbell unrung. Persistence is the key to selling. Success is a matter of living, breathing, sweating without pause. This is the truth Steve Sklar preaches. He has little tolerance for other vacuum cleaner salesmen who preach gimmicks. Offer the lady of the house a chance to win a free trip to Hawaii, they'll say, or how about a free rug shampoo? Do anything, they'll say, just get your foot in the door. Sklar says, sure, he could get his foot in a lot of doors.

"But it don't mean diddly-squat."

Diddly-squat to Sklar means finding a person he can work with. "I'm not gonna fool the people with gimmicks," he says. "That, to me, lowers you like a dog. That, to me, is like puttin' your tail between your legs, like a dog. I won't allow it for myself, okay?"

And so vacuum cleaner selling to Sklar is, instead, rather like fishing: Keep your line out long enough, and a big one's bound to come along.

Yesterday, he hooked a lady in Northwest who had a sick Eureka. She also had a big barking dog in her backyard, plus a very skinny cat with hardly any hair on it—it was very possibly the skinniest, frailest cat alive in America today—plus a baby in a Swyngomatic, rocking gleefully, automatically. Holding her sick

Eureka, the lady said, "Yes," she would love a demo of a new Electrolux, and so Sklar went out to his van to retrieve his machinery. "She's a cool lady. A cute gal. I like her," he was saying, all excited. And then he went into her living room, and he did it up good. He sat on the piano bench and explained all the features of the new Electrolux "Marquise." He turned on the machine and pulled massive dirt balls out of the lady's carpet, thus showing her all the dirt her old Eureka had failed to suck up. He pulled more enormous balls of dirt out of her furniture, saying, "It's one thing to walk on dirt, it's another thing to sit on dirt." And then, as if in a vacuuming frenzy, he proceeded to take on the curtains, the wood floor, the windowsills, while the woman just sat there smiling, and the baby went to and fro, and the cat watched suspiciously. He showed the lady how easy it is to change the bags, and he showed her the retractable cord, pulling it clear out 20 feet, then releasing it and letting it go "snap!" back into place, which sent the skinny, hairless cat darting into the bathroom for fear of its life, so shocked was it by this magic. Indeed, Sklar gave the entire show, and his performance was positively excellent, but in the end the woman spit out the hook. "Yeah, well, I'll have to ask my husband," she said.

Leaving, Sklar said he was not upset by this setback, but you could see angry sweat on his brow. "Idiot!" he said, finally, and he wasn't referring to himself.

Then he said: "I don't know. I'm thinking later of going into real estate."

Late in life, Steve Sklar's father quit the Fuller Brush Company and went into insurance.

"No, I don't know what his problem totally was," he'll say about his father, wondering why the old man didn't make it as an ace Fuller Brush salesman. Sklar talks a lot about his father while he walks.

And he walks. He rings doorbells. He sucks on sugarless candy. He opens storm doors, knocks, tramples over lawns. Finally, a lady answers. He starts to give his pitch, but before he can get the word "Electrolux" out of his mouth, the lady gets excited. "I REALLY COULDN'T DEAL WITH ANYTHING MORE TODAY," she shouts, all nervous and apparently wrapped up in something horribly stressful. "I'm just too caught up . . . I REALLY COULDN'T DEAL . . .," she says, shutting the door, and Steve Sklar says, "Fool!" and then goes on walking. He mutters about his job. He mutters like a man mad at his job. He mutters like a man mad at what has happened to the world.

"Today, when you come to the door, the lady's like, 'Hey, you're infringing upon my privacy.' It's a big difference from the way it used to be. In the golden era. It used to be, 'Oh, come in, let me see what you got.' You were a nice break in the lady's day.

"You were the Prince of Merchandise.

"Now, you're just a pain in the ass," he says. "The reception is gone. People are afraid, they're busy, they don't give a damn no more about people coming to the door. They go to the shopping mall to buy their damn stuff. They don't need me. She don't need me. I'm just a pest coming to her door now, okay? No, I'm serious. I'm being candid," he says, ringing another doorbell.

The door opens.

". . . Hello, there, how are you today, sir? I bet the lady of the house uses Electrolux, does she? We're just in the area servicing them . . ."

"She just died," the man says, and when Steve Sklar says, "I'm sorry to hear that, sir . . . Uh, what type of vacuum do you have?" the man shuts the door. "Crazy man!" Sklar mutters, turning away, and he continues walking. He mutters about his job. He mutters about the world. He mutters about his father. He mutters about himself.

"My father, well, he liked to read books, okay? I don't think he liked selling. He couldn't inspire himself. He was just sort of a . . . heavy person. You know how some people are heavy, just, sorta, they're just sorta heavy mentally? They get dragged down on all the complexities of the world," he says, and rings another doorbell.

And it's a hit.

He strikes up a conversation with the lady. She is a kindred soul: She owns an Electrolux. And, yes, she likes it very much, thank you. Sklar offers to check her Electrolux, to make sure it's working okay, and she says, "How much will it cost?" and he says, "No charge," and she says, "Come right in." And so he looks at her vacuum cleaner, and the housekeeper comes out to look at the vacuum cleaner, and so does the lady's young son, who is home sick from school, and suddenly everybody grows very concerned about the vacuum cleaner, especially when Sklar opens the machine up, runs his finger along one opening, then looks at his finger. "Oh, dear," he says. "Oh, my." He pauses. He sighs. The people look at him. "You gotta bunch of burnt material coming out of this motor," he says, finally.

"A bunch of what?"

"Burnt material," he says, informing the family that their vacuum cleaner is, in fact, very sick.

"What! How can you tell?"

"There's black stuff coming out," he says.

"Oh, for godsakes," the woman says. "This is horrible. This is just horrible!" She runs her hands through her hair. Her day is now officially ruined.

Sklar looks at the woman, and there is condolence in his eyes. The woman had no idea her vacuum cleaner was bad. The woman had no idea she had a problem until Steve Sklar knocked at her door. Indeed, this woman had no idea that she is a fish, and that this stranger is a fisherman, and she has just swallowed a hook.

"How many times does the machine get used, ma'am?" Sklar asks.

"Well, once a week very heavily. And another time the children's rooms," she says.

"Heavily . . . the children's rooms . . . uh-huh, you've had this, what, seven, eight years?"

"Yes."

"It's got about 16–20 years' use on it."

The woman appears quite insulted by this remark. She shoots a glance at the housekeeper. She says, "Well, she is very hard on equipment . . . ," and the housekeeper disappears into the kitchen.

"Keep your fingers out of there!" the lady shouts at her son, who has his hand in the vacuum cleaner motor, where the black stuff is coming out.

"Yeah, you don't need to put your hands in there, son," Sklar says. He tells the woman that he will go outside and get his "tester." He says then, and only then, can he ascertain the true trouble with her machine.

"Keep your hands out of there," the lady says to the boy again.

"Yeah, you don't need to do that, son."

"Would you wash your hands please? Now!"

"Why?" the boy asks.

"Because it's GUCK!" she shouts, while Sklar goes out to his van to get his "tester."

He is excited. He is a man rejuvenated. With gusto, he takes a brand new machine out of a box and proceeds to assemble it, there, in the lady's driveway. Sklar uses this strategy often. He will bring a brand new machine into a house, and he will call it his "tester." And he will show the lady how great the tester sucks up dirt, especially when compared with her old machine—a Hoover, a Eureka, an Electrolux, it matters not what kind of machine.

Steve Sklar will give a free checkup on any make or model. And each time, he says, "Let me go get my tester." And he'll let you try his tester, let you get the feel of it. And he will let your housekeeper try the tester, your mother, your husband; vacuuming can be fun for the whole family, especially with a machine as beautiful as this tester. What? You say you want to buy this tester? Well. . . .

"And then in the end," Sklar concludes, "I can just go, 'Do you want this machine, or shall I give you one in a new box?' And it's a close."

And so, inside, suddenly, Steve Sklar's vacuum cleaner testing act turns into a magic moment of salesmanship.

"Jiminy Cricket!" he shouts, and with that he reveals a great ball of dirt. "Holy Toledo!" he says. "See what your old machine is leaving?"

The woman appears to be most disheartened. Here she was, going about her life, believing her house was clean. And here this man comes out of nowhere, plugs in a vacuum cleaner and destroys her whole happy illusion.

And here he is trying to sell her a new illusion. It will cost her $699, the theory being that if you pay a lot of money now, you will never again have to worry about dirt; the principle Steve Sklar sells is that the more you invest today, the freer and safer you will be tomorrow. Freedom from dirt balls. Safety from a mattress full of microscopic bugs nibbling at your dead skin, according to a poster hanging in an Electrolux office in Washington. Freedom! Safety! Who doesn't want these things?

Apparently, this lady doesn't. In the end, she doesn't buy; instead she opts to get a $200 overhaul on her old machine. "Don't sniffle on the man!" she shouts to her son as Steve Sklar packs up all of his equipment and takes it out of the house. He is silent. He wraps the hoses up and tucks all the machinery just so, back into its boxes, like puppets being put to bed. Finally, he blurts: "Baloney-head!" And he isn't referring to himself.

He gets in the van. He is silent. Angry. Pensive. He is fed up. From the dashboard, he takes out a tape recorder. He turns it on. He puts it on the seat between his legs. He heads over to Virginia to deliver some bags. He mutters louder than the voice coming out of the tape recorder. He mutters about life. He mutters about fools, crazy men, baloney-heads. "I didn't impress her enough with the dirt . . . the whole key is: How do they react to the dirt?" He mutters about his father. "He's cool, though, really. I love the man. High integrity, man, one thing I'll say." He mutters about himself. "Me, I'm like a damn fraud compared to him. He has integrity to a T. He would not do some of the things I do in selling. Me, I'll do certain stuff to a certain T in order to put food on the table. In other words, I'll take a little old lady, and I'll sell her a new machine whether she needs it or not—if she's got a lot of money. Because I figure, let her spend the money on me. I'm worth it. I'm young. I've got a family to raise. My father would not do that." He takes out a sugarless candy and sucks on it.

And, at last, he listens to the tape recorder. The voice coming out of it is his real estate teacher—two nights a week Steve Sklar goes to learn about real estate. He records every word emitted from the mouth of his real estate teacher. He is silent. He listens to the tape the way a man might read the Bible—with allegiance, hope, praise. "If this is the tax rate per dollar, you take the tax rate and multiply it by the assessed value," the voice coming out from between his legs says. And Steve Sklar says, "Man, this is beautiful. This guy is recharged. He is rejuvenated.

"He is reborn," he says, as if God Himself has come down in the form of some real estate teacher, some wizard, and as if the American dream itself were some vacuum cleaner. It is old, and it just isn't picking up the way it used to. There is black stuff coming out of it. Burnt material. GUCK! The motor is burning itself up. Maybe it's time for an overhaul, or maybe it's time to invest in a whole new illusion.

Magic | 2

Legend has it that Colon, Michigan, doesn't exist, except for four days each August, when the magicians appear. More than 1,000 magicians from all over the world have been congregating here for the past 54 years, doubling the population of Colon, a town named after the punctuation mark. Colon is one of those places you stop and rest in—but not with quite the same conviction and duration as you would, say, at a period.

In Colon there are no traffic lights, no fast food chains, no shopping malls, and No Parking on Any Street from 2 A.M. until 6 A.M., the signs say. There is a hardware store (Magic City Hardware), a Beauty Parlor (Illusions Hair Care), a defunct health club (Magic City Fitness Centre), a baseball team called the Magi, and a main street lined with flower pots that look like giant top hats. Colon also has a museum where you can see pictures of Harry Blackstone Sr., the late, great, world-famous magician who lived here from 1925 until 1965. Blackstone attracted a following of magicians, and he helped start what is now Abbott's Magic Manufacturing Company, the largest magic manufacturer in the world. It's still here in Colon, inside a low black building decorated with dancing skeletons.

Thanks to Blackstone, and thanks to Abbott's, Colon became known as the Magic Capital of the World.

The magicians come here as if it were their mecca, raising Cain for four days, and then they all vanish. When that happens, some say, Colon vanishes too, only to reappear the following August when the magicians return.

People who live here say no, that's not true. But then again, what do they know? Maybe the locals don't exist either, except for four days each August. Life in Colon is mysterious, all right. Mystery is what lends significance to this seemingly insignificant place, a compact town, threaded by route 86 and bordered on either end by giant water sprinklers shooting in spasms over cornfields headed forever into the horizon.

"Now, remember, I'm not God," is a common disclaimer you hear in Colon during the Magic Get Together. This is important. A magician will say this before performing a trick so as to assure you of his flesh and blood status. Magicians consider themselves entertainers, nothing more. None of these people pretend to have supernatural powers. People who make such claims are not allowed into the brotherhood of magicians, because they are not abiding by the honor code. Inside the brotherhood, magicians share tricks with generosity and pride. The reason they never reveal tricks to outsiders is, simply, because they have sworn to one another that they never would. Magicians have a heightened sense of honor. Magicians are some of the happiest people you will ever in your life meet.

"Hey, watch this," is another common thing you hear in Colon during the Magic Get-Together.

"Hey, watch this," says a man who blows a bubble, then catches the bubble, turns the bubble into a solid ball, bounces the ball, turns it back into a bubble, and pops it. And then he leaves.

"Hey, watch this," says another, who takes a quarter from you, sticks his cigarette through it, smokes the cigarette as it sits there stuck through your quarter, returns your quarter, and then he leaves.

"Hey, watch this," says yet another, who performs a simple sponge ball routine, and then, just as he is about to leave, reveals the fact that your wrist watch is inside his pocket.

It goes on like this. There are magic shows, magic lectures, magic tricks for sale, jugglers, ventriloquists and levitating bodies all over the streets and diners and lawns of Colon. Still, most of the action happens in the high school, which is air conditioned.

"It's cute, I'm telling you," says Jack Bridwell, a magic salesman. He is out here just across from the home-ec room, where tables have been set up for people to sell tricks. He is presently demonstrating a flower routine to Aaron Olson, a 16-year-old magician from Ripon, Wisconsin.

"This bo-kay comes loose, see?" says Jack. "Now you say, 'I'm going to water the plant' . . . and three snakes pop out! Oh, it's a beautiful thing. 'Abbott's Gufus Plant' we call it. Whoops, just a little dust on that, see, it comes right off. . . ."

Aaron is not convinced. He's looking for something a little more dramatic.

"Last month I vanished a fire truck," announces Aaron. (The word "vanish," enjoys a special usage in magic language. One does not "make something vanish." One "vanishes something.") Aaron has been doing magic tricks since he was three years old. "And I can't stop. It's almost like a drug. I won't be able to stop. I'll be doing tricks until the day I die." Vanishing the fire truck—which he did in front of 4,000 people—was a lifetime achievement. "I cried," he says. "I cried for two days. I was just so moved."

Next year, Aaron hopes to saw a fire truck in half.

"Cool," says Franz Harary, a 30-year-old magician standing by. The two have just met. Franz is famous. Franz did all of the effects for Michael Jackson's "Victory" tour. Soon, Franz hopes to vanish a Las Vegas casino, saying he's using a new technique that enables him to vanish virtually anything. "I could vanish Long Island," says Franz.

"Cool," says Aaron.

Franz says Aaron shouldn't saw a fire truck in half, though. "You'll get known as 'that fire truck guy,'" says Franz. "You should do a ship or a chopper."

Aaron considers this. "How about the Concorde?"

"Excellent," says Franz. "Saw the Concorde in half and then you'll be somebody."

Aaron walks away, shaking his head, saying you just can't get advice like this in Ripon, Wisconsin.

Later, Franz goes out and levitates a lady over a lake.

Young magicians come to Colon to meet their idols, to get energized, to plan newer and more amazing feats. Old magicians come to Colon to look back and revel in a life worth living.

Both forces come together at the cemetery, where old and young alike congregate. Just off route 86, the cemetery is generally considered Colon's main attraction. Magicians are buried here, all of their gravestones spread out like an audience surrounding the great stone of Harry Blackstone himself.

"It's a flame."

"It's a tulip."

"It's a phallic symbol."

"No, it's a flame." People wonder what Blackstone's gravestone is actually supposed to represent. It's a big oval thing sticking up in the air. Terry Seabrooke, a veteran British magician, is out here taking pictures of it. Most magicians who come to Colon do this. Terry does magic tricks for, among other audiences, the Queen of England. Dukes and princes and princesses gather around the Buckingham Palace ballroom and sit at Terry's feet. Still, his favorite place to come is Colon.

"Because this is more off the wall than anything that ever was," says Terry. His two friends, Mercer Helms and George Jackstone, agree. Mercer used to do the warm-up show for Phyllis Diller. George got his training as an assistant to Blackstone, and then went on to do the warm-up show for Elvis Presley.

The three aging magicians wander through the cemetery, looking for their friends: here's the "Amazing Conklins," here's "Shorty," here's "Bill Baird the Magnificent Fraud."

George says he wants to end up here, too. "With me, they're going to split my ashes," he says. "Half is going in Chicago with my wife, and then somebody's going to do a dirty trick with a spade and dump the rest of me here with Harry."

Terry: "I'll pour a bottle of scotch over you."

Mercer: "Hey, here's a stone for Little Johnny Jones. . . . He's not even dead yet."

Terry: "Poor bloke. He must be very uncomfortable."

The three men continue to poke though the cemetery, sharing memories, kidding one another, at times doubling over with laughter in the dry August air. Mercer bends down, arranges some flowers around a friend. "The thing is," he says. "It's the only happy cemetery I've ever been to. Have you noticed the happiness here?"

When the big evening magic show finally begins, all the bleachers and the entire basketball court of the Colon High School gym are filled with people. This house has been sold out, in fact, for years. Young people in the back. Old people up front. The generations move this way. You wait until someone dies to get closer up. Looking from back to front is like looking at the movement of time.

Backstage is a manic scene of glitter and gold and rabbits and doves in cages, and people sweating, and giant boxes and chain saws whizzing to and fro. And there are dogs dressed as tigers. And a pig dressed as a rhinoceros. And two men dressed in drag poking these animals around, their magic act based on the theory that everyone loves an identity crisis.

Standing alone, ready to go on, is Earl Ray Wilcox. His small table rests on a few rickety wheels. He has a top hat. And no other props. He is an old man who still looks young, and it is in this solitary figure that you can get a glimpse of why, in the end, magicians have such happy souls.

"I don't have anything hooked on my body or nothing," explains Earl. "Fifteen years ago I had an act with gadgets all over me. But I scrapped it. Too much crap to deal with. I thought, 'Hey, a real magician wouldn't do that.'"

Sandwiched between acts of fire and glitter and birds and hidden wires, Earl comes on stage alone.

He says nothing. He looks at his audience. Suddenly, he pulls a coin out of the air, looking himself surprised to find it there. He pulls more coins out of the air, more, and more, and more, filling up an entire bucket with half-dollars. He pulls cards out of the air. He pulls coins and cards from his feet. He is graceful. He is balletic. He pulls cards from his mouth, turns them into giant cards, turns them into jumbo cards. Flawlessly, Earl seems to dance with his own magic.

The people applaud respectfully, like you do at the symphony.

"Well, I'm done," says Earl, coming backstage. "I'm relieved. I'm hungry. I want a drink. Oh, it's a big happiness." He is dripping with sweat. One drop hangs on the end of each ear lobe. "You actually get yourself into a high out there, doing magic," he says. "I do. It's a hard feeling to describe. It's unique. I go out there and I say, 'Hey, I'm a magician.' I am going to do things that can't be done. I say 'Hey, I am going to pull coins out of the air.' And I really believe I'm doing it.

"For 11 minutes I actually believe in myself."

Afterwards, all the magicians go to the Legion, post 454. They drink beer out of plastic cups, and eat hamburgers presented to them on paper plates each garnished with a cherry tomato rolling uncontrollably. And long into the night everyone does magic tricks—Aaron, Franz, Terry, George, Mercer—all the magicians are here. Except for Earl Ray Wilcox, who is done, this day, believing in himself.

Maybe Earl doesn't exist, except during those 11 minutes of belief. Maybe it all works this way.

The Balloon Lady 3

It was a wild idea: a hot-air balloon shaped like a giant bell. A bronze bell, with a crack. It was a fantastic idea! A giant Liberty Bell. A flying Liberty Bell. A great, big, gigantic Liberty Bell, carrying an old lady across the sky.

Actually, the Liberty Bell was Mrs. Wolf's second idea. What she really wanted was a balloon shaped like Independence Hall— imagine that, Independence Hall soaring over your house—but by the time she came up with this hare-brained scheme, there wasn't time. It would take more than a year to make a balloon in the shape of Independence Hall. But she could get a Liberty Bell balloon made in a quick six months, for a mere $100,000.

Money was no object, since Mrs. Wolf is paying for this thing herself. It is her way of saying "Happy Birthday" to the U.S. Constitution. If all goes according to plan, while Philadelphia celebrates the bicentennial of the signing of that momentous document, Mrs. Wolf will be flying over the city of Philadelphia, in a hot-air balloon shaped like the Liberty Bell.

The city of Philadelphia did not ask Mrs. Wolf to do this. Nor did anyone ask her to fly in one of her balloons in 1976 to help kick off the nation's bicentennial. Nor did they ask her, in 1982, to pay $20,000 for a balloon with William Penn's picture on it and fly it over Philadelphia, then celebrating its tricentennial. No, City Hall did not ask Mrs. Wolf to do any of this. Usually city officials try to discourage her. Maybe because they think she's too old to be flying in balloons. Maybe because they think she's just plain bonkers.

Her full name is Constance Wolf. She is 82 years old. She wears a black veil across her face. She is a world-champion balloonist, and her life has been a series of these things, a series of hare-brained schemes.

"This, my dear, this is going to work," Connie Wolf says to me. She is holding a piece of the bronze-colored material that she has chosen for the Liberty Bell balloon. "Nothing is going to stop me from doing this," she says. She's been so angry at the city of Philadelphia for not paying attention to her gifts. But she is going to try again. "This has just got to work," she says.

We are sitting in the parlor of the eighteenth century farmhouse in Blue Bell where Connie Wolf lives alone. We are here, sipping tea, as we have been, on and off, for the last five years. This is the way it works: Connie Wolf sits in the triangular chair, complaining about her aching knees, and she looks off to the window and recalls story after story about her life up inside the clouds. Connie Wolf has been flying balloons since 1952 and airplanes since 1931. She is one of seven female pilots in the world to hold a valid pilot's license for 50 years or more.

Primarily, she is a gas balloonist—not a hot-air balloonist, she is quick to point out. This is the far lovelier sport: bouncing through the air beneath a ball of hydrogen. You don't see many gas balloons around anymore; people tend to fear them. "It's a national guilt complex, on account of the Hindenberg," Connie Wolf will tell you, adding, "Gas ballooning is no more dangerous than anything else you do—just don't rub your hind legs together."

Connie Wolf was the first woman, and first American, to pilot a gas balloon over the Swiss Alps; she once broke 15 world records in a gas balloon, ten of which she holds today. Of all the balloons she has ever piloted, her favorite was probably La Coquette, the one she and her balloon club lent to Mike Todd so that he could use it in his film *Around the World in Eighty Days*. Connie Wolf soared over Paris in La Coquette, promoting the film. She drifted over London, too, "and I almost landed at Buckingham Palace, but I didn't have the nerve."

That was the way it went: Connie Wolf sat in the triangular chair, and she told me stories about balloons. They were funny stories. I would roll over on the soft down couch, laughing, looking at this old lady with the veil across her face and wishing I could climb inside her life, as in a balloon, and soar away from normalcy forever.

Imagine shaking hands with Richard Nixon and then taking off over the city of Chester in a balloon bearing his name. This is 1960. Connie loves Vice President Richard Nixon. She wants him to be president. He wants to be president, too. (To this day, Connie Wolf keeps a photograph of Nixon on her dining room table. "And every time I walk by, I give him a little love tap. I can ruin almost anyone's meal with that picture.")

Four thousand people are here, looking up at the balloon with Richard Nixon's name written all over it. One local Republican of some weight, so undone by the sight, decides she wants to go along for the balloon ride. She really is of some weight. Connie Wolf is mad. "I can't take any more weight!" she says, but the woman hops in anyway. They take off, soaring somewhat clumsily above the Delaware River, the balloon with Richard Nixon's name written all over it now looking like a giant campaign button pinned to the sky. On the ground, Richard and Pat Nixon—Pat is looking smart in a pillbox hat—plus the 4,000 other people, are waving.

Up in the air, the local Republican gags. "HA!" she says and then announces, with some difficulty, that she has only one lung. Soaring 2,000 feet above the Delaware River, this woman of some weight cannot breathe. Emergency! Connie Wolf tries to land the balloon.

Sadness awaits below. The balloon is headed for a cemetery. There is a funeral going on. Connie Wolf is hovering over this funeral, throwing out sand, trying to avoid it. The mourners are not amused. Above them, an old lady in a veil is flying in a balloon with Richard Nixon's name written all over it and is bombing their funeral service with sand. The mourners scatter right and left. The weighty one-lunged Republican is saying, "HA."

Connie Wolf decides to get a picture of this. Nobody would ever believe it. She picks up her camera—her prized three-dimensional camera—and before she can click the shutter, she slips, rights herself, then drops the camera overboard. The balloon shoots up like a rocket, and Connie Wolf cannot believe her eyes. The one-lunged Republican, noting abrupt changes in altitude more severely than most, says "HAAAAAA!"

According to a story in the *Evening Bulletin* a few days later, Connie Wolf's camera landed six feet from two florists hard at work in the cemetery's greenhouse, the roof of which was shattered to smithereens. "The war must have started," one florist is quoted as having said. "This must be it." "Bombing the Greenhouse" was the headline of that *Bulletin* story, and it is but a chapter in the lifelong comedy of errors that defines Connie Wolf.

In her parlor, Connie Wolf says, "It's my nickel and it's a sensational thing and I know it." She is talking about the Liberty Bell balloon, and she is excited. "This is going to work," she says again. She says she hopes people in Philadelphia pay attention to her gift this time, since this probably is the last hare-brained scheme of her life.

"It's so unlikely that I should still be around," she says. "I fully expected to die a few years ago. Seriously. I don't know if I told you that. I was devastated by Alfred Wolf's death, and I fully expected to die." Alfred Wolf was her husband of 54 years.

"And I'm going to make this Liberty Bell thing work. Nothing can spoil it. Nothing. I'm living from week to week. Literally. And I feel that I haven't lived in vain if I can do something important with this story."

The "story" Connie Wolf is talking about is only incidentally the story of the Liberty Bell balloon, or the Nixon balloon, or the William Penn balloon, or La Coquette, or any of the others. The story is much bigger than these. It has to do with Alfred Wolf— people called him "Abby"—and it has to do with the sky.

"My poor head," Connie Wolf said. This was a few years ago. She rose slowly, feebly. It was always such a chore, getting up from the triangular chair, what with her "crackly old knees," and now here she had a headache, too. "I fell down somebody's cellar steps and bonked my head. My poor head," she said, and then went to go call Abby. He was working upstairs, and we were downstairs, hungry. We were supposed to go to the club for lunch.

She had on her veil. It was a mask made of a very thin mesh material, like a hair net, that she had stretched around her entire face, then tied in a bow behind her head. It didn't conceal her features. The effect was dainty, like the wrapper on a new China doll. "It keeps my head on," she would say, to some people who ask. To others she explains simply, "I think it looks attractive. Don't you think it looks attractive?"

"AAABBBBYY!" she hollered. The voice hardly belonged to a feeble old woman. "AAAABBBBYYY!" she yelled, and then turned to me. "You know, he's nearly deaf," she said. "And you know, he doesn't really care for balloons. It's only fair to tell you.

"Alfred Wolf really would not care for us to discuss balloons in front of him."

The day was hot and hopelessly humid. It was August. Connie Wolf was wearing a pair of pink and green and orange and blue flowered trousers—"psychedelic," you might say—that were short, flapping now and again, high above a pair of navy blue Keds. She had just come inside from cutting the grass, sitting atop a huge red farm tractor circa 1947. Wingover, as the Wolf estate is called, is 50 acres of prime real estate in Blue Bell. The grass Connie Wolf had just finished cutting was, in actual fact, a runway, her husband's runway. There was an airplane tied to the ground, just by the apple trees. From high atop her red farm tractor, Connie Wolf groomed the runway low and smooth for Alfred Wolf, who would take off from it and land on it in his Cessna 170.

"My poor head," Connie Wolf said again. "I got a concussion," she said, "when I bonked my head, when I fell down those horrible steps.

"ABBYYY!" she called again. He wasn't answering. "Now remember," she said to me. "When Alfred Wolf comes downstairs, we really must stop talking about balloons."

That was the rule. When Abby was around, balloons were out. Alfred Wolf was a retired Air Force brigadier general, a jet pilot, a world-renowned aviation attorney—senior partner in the firm Wolf, Block, Schorr & Solis-Cohen in Philadelphia. He was also an accomplished archaeological scuba diver for the Academy of Natural Sciences. He once led an expedition that recovered Capt. Cook's jettisoned cannon. He was also a professor of aviation law. And he was also, perhaps first and foremost, cofounder and secretary of AOPA—the Aircraft Owners and Pilots Association—an international organization of more than 220,000 pilots from 22 nations.

That was the rule. When Abby was around, Abby was the star. "He's the more active of the two of us," Connie would say. "Oh, I just stooge for him; that's what my life is. I don't work or do anything. I cut the grass. I wash his socks. I wait the tables. And he hates it. Because he thinks I should be off leading the world or something. He absolutely hates it.

"And so that was where the balloon came in as a wonderful weapon," she said, and she looked at me, expecting me to understand all of this. "Getting in a balloon," she said, "it was the only way I could flatten Abby out.

"AAAAABBBYY!" she hollered again. "Oh, my poor head," she said, turning to me. "My hairdresser was feeling around this morning to see if there were any new sprouts. I got scalped, you see, when I got the concussion, when I fell down those horrible steps. My hairdresser said: 'No, it's still scalped.'

"AAABBBYY!" she said one last time, and it became apparent that it was hopeless for now. So for now, at least, we could spend a few more moments talking about balloons.

Pick an adventure, any adventure. Connie Wolf fans them out like a deck of cards. Once, she took a world record away from Russia. This was in 1961. Connie Wolf hated Russia—just about as much as she loved Richard Nixon. We were in a Cold War situation. Russia was winning all the above-ground battles. First, in October of 1957—just four months before we were supposed to launch the world's first artificial Earth satellite—they sent up

Sputnik I. Then, in January 1959—just two months before we were supposed to put the first satellite in orbit around the sun—they did it with Mechta I. This was getting ridiculous. Finally, in 1960, we came out with the Mercury-Atlas vehicle: a rocket with a capsule on top, designed to carry a man into orbit. This was it! We were going to be the first to send a real live human being into space. We were feeling so proud, so brave, so American.

NASA put on a demonstration. The countdown began. Everybody was watching. Just off the launch pad, the Mercury-Atlas vehicle blew up.

On April 12, 1961, Soviet cosmonaut Yuri Gagarin was the first man in orbit.

Connie Wolf was sick of the whole mess. It is now November 1961. She picks a nice, flat, windless town called Big Spring, Texas. She arrives with a balloon plus a bottle of "goofballs." She is popping these amphetamines like Chiclets. The people in Big Spring have no idea what this woman with the veil and the big silver flight suit is all about. This is not a publicized event. It wasn't in the papers. It is sponsored by no one. This 56-year-old woman just arrived, said she wanted to stay up in a balloon for two days, then go home.

She did it. Plopping down in a cornfield in Boley, Oklahoma, on Nov. 20, 1961, Connie Wolf had a six-hour edge over two Russian women who set the record in 1948 for endurance in a free balloon. Connie Wolf was up there, in the sky, alone with her goofballs, for 40 hours and 13 minutes. As an unexpected little bonus, she broke 14 other world records during that flight, including one for altitude—13,597 feet—and another for distance. She traveled 350 miles, farther than any woman had ever gone in a gas balloon.

"Just to prove that one capitalist can take on two Communists any day," was the quote that went over the wires. It was hot news in 1961. People called it a "Cold War feat." The *Detroit Free Press* called Connie Wolf one of the female newsmakers of 1961—along with Jacqueline Kennedy, Princess Margaret, Marilyn Monroe and Joan Sutherland. The *Miami News* said: "It wasn't a feat to compare with orbiting the Earth in space or tripling the speed of sound in a rocket ship, but somehow we all feel a little better for Mrs. Wolf having done it."

Later, in Athens, Greece, the Federation Aeronautique Internationale named Connie Wolf the winner of the 1961 Montgolfier Award, the most coveted award in ballooning. Before Connie Wolf, it had never gone to a woman, nor to an American.

"My poor head," Connie Wolf said again, looking at me. "I got sunburn on it, when I was cutting the grass. Sunburn on the part where I got scalped, when I got the concussion, when I fell down those horrible steps. My poor head."

"ABBBYY," she called. We were really hungry.

"AABBYY," she said, and this time he answered. "Are you all right dear?" she asked.

"No, dear, I'm horrible," he said. "I may not live."

"Poor dear," she said, then asked him to please hurry so that we could eat. "The club" was the restaurant at Wings Field, a private airport next to the Wolfs' property. Brig. Gen. Alfred Wolf would be dining with us there, and so that was it: No more balloon talk.

He said he wanted to fly his airplane to the club. She said she wanted to drive her car. They put me in the airplane.

It was loud. It was old. It went rumbling down the grassy runway toward the club, and finally it took us up, higher, then higher, and by the time we were fully up in the sky, the club was gone. The club was behind us. The club was, after all, just across the street from the Wolfs'. That was the way it worked with Alfred Wolf: When in doubt, fly. Fly anywhere. Fly everywhere. Fly across the street.

Alfred Wolf taught Connie Wolf how to fly airplanes—on their honeymoon. Twenty years later, in 1951, Abby took Connie on her first balloon ride. It was his first balloon ride, too. This was over Zurich. Looking down, Connie Wolf never took such beautiful pictures in her life. This was positively fantastic! Abby wasn't quite so enthralled. He was not enjoying the splendor of the countryside below. "He was terrified," Connie Wolf will tell you. "He was huddled at the bottom of this miserable laundry basket." He was looking at a feather. The feather was attached to the end of a string. It was beside the basket, dangling in the air. When the balloon went down, the feather went up, and vice versa. That was the way it worked in the old gas balloons: Your gauge was a feather. Accustomed to more sophisticated instruments, Alfred Wolf couldn't quite deal with the feather. It was a question of precision. He never forgot the feather. Brig. Gen. Alfred L. Wolf, a man who would go on to fly just about anything potentially airborne—from the flying machines of '29 to multi-Mach fighters, giant transports, helicopters and seaplanes—swore that day that he would never again set foot in a balloon, and he never did.

At the club, Abby had eggs and chocolate milk. Connie lifted her veil and nibbled at mushrooms stuffed with crabmeat. We watched the airplanes. It was here at Wings Field that Alfred Wolf, along with four other pilots, started AOPA in 1938. The idea was to give the private pilot—the grassroots flier—a voice. As Alfred Wolf put it: "AOPA was founded in a defensive way." As Connie Wolf put it: "We were being pushed out of the sky!"

In the 1920s and 1930s, when the sky was becoming a new highway, and everybody was up there trying it out—the airlines, the military and the private pilots, too—regulations were quickly being formed. The airlines and the military, the big trucks and buses of the sky, had strong lobbies. And compared to them, the private pilots were like kids on bicycles, skinny pipsqueaks, getting pushed off to the curb. So, they got together.

As Alfred Wolf put it: "Today, AOPA is such a huge organization, we no longer are on the defensive. Today, we encode the regulations." As Connie Wolf put it: "Imagine that! Twenty-two nations, 220,000 pilots, all of them together because of my husband!"

This is what his life was devoted to: a safe and happy and affordable place in the sky for everyone. The sky belongs to everyone. And this is what her life was devoted to: Promoting Abby. That was how it went.

When Connie Wolf made her dramatic balloon flights in 1976 and 1982 over the city of Philadelphia, she was only in part paying homage to a nation's bicentennial and a city's tricentennial. Both years, she made these flights on January 9. It was an important anniversary. It marked the day flight was inaugurated in North America. Jean Pierre Blanchard piloted a hydrogen balloon from Sixth and Walnut Streets in Philadelphia to Woodbury, New Jersey, on January 9, 1793. Connie Wolf made repeat performances of this hallmark journey, thus promoting aviation, promoting the sky, promoting Abby's passion.

Abby gulped down his chocolate milk, gulped it down good. Lunch was over. He went to his airplane, and she went to her car. They put me in the car.

It was old. It was creaky. It was a Mustang convertible, circa 1965. The sun was beating down on Mrs. Wolf's head. Her poor head. She didn't want any more sunburn on the part that was scalped, thanks to the concussion, thanks to the tumble down those horrible steps. She didn't have a hat. She had a box of tissues. She jammed the box of tissues onto her head, jammed it down tight. She turned to look at me. I looked at her, this woman with the psychedelic pants and the veil across her face and the box of tissues on her head.

"Am I embarrassing you?" she asked. The tissues got her thinking of Howard Hughes, how he used to wear boxes of tissues on his feet. "Poor Howard Hughes," she said. "I just feel so terribly about the way he was treated. And I helped. One time I wrote him a note and said I'd like to stay with him and work for him; I hurt his feelings. He thought I wanted to stay there because I loved him. Oh, I broke his heart," she said.

Before she met Abby, Connie was a theatrical agent in New York. It's how she knew all the stars—people like Mike Todd, Elizabeth Taylor, Brian Aherne, Ginger Rogers, Arthur Godfrey, Howard Hughes and others. They were "great friends" of the Wolfs. Some of them would come to the Wolfs' for parties. There were the famous "fly-in" parties. As many as 150 airplanes would come and land on the Wolfs' runway. The people would play badminton in the barn and press apples for apple wine, and sometimes they would convert the badminton court into a movie house, and the Hollywood stars would preview their movies.

"Abby will kill me if he knows I'm doing this," Connie said. We were in the car. We were sneaking through a gate at Wings Field, where cars are forbidden. The gate opened onto a runway. "Abby would absolutely kill me if he knew," she said. We zoomed down the runway, then hid behind an airplane.

There was Abby. We were spying on him. He was climbing into his airplane. "Poor Abby," Connie said. "No one's here to see him off," she said. We were, apparently, here to wish Abby a grand "bon voyage!" on this, his journey across the street.

"You know," she said, sighing, waiting for takeoff, "he really does not want me being a tweeny, a servant, a lawnmower, anything like that around the place. He says: 'You got the money to pay for things, why don't you hire people?' But I want to look after him. It's all I really want to do. And it is so aggravating to him.

"Don't you see?" she said, turning to me. The box of tissues had slid over toward one ear. "Whenever Abby got too repulsive to me about how I was not fulfilling my destiny as a leader in this world, or whatever, I would haul out a balloon. And it would flatten him out. It would keep him quiet."

She told me a secret. It was about her "Cold War feat" over Big Spring, Texas. This was not her hare-brained scheme; it was Abby's. He talked her into it. He was very insistent. "Just go get a world record!" he had said. What he never told her, however, was that while she was off trying to steal a world record away from the Russians, he would be down at the Hospital of the University of Pennsylvania, getting his intestines worked over. She was obsessed enough with washing his stupid socks; there was no telling what she might do with his intestinal polyps.

So, he sent her off to get a world record. The first attempt, in Indianapolis, failed. Connie Wolf came home to Blue Bell, dejected. "Where's Abby!" she shouted. Abby wasn't home. She found him in the hospital. "And he looked so pitiful, and he had all these tubes coming out of him, and I said: 'You're breaking my heart! Why didn't you tell me? You're breaking my heart!' And he said—and it took him a good half hour to get this out—he said, 'You want to make me feel better?' he said, 'I like a balloonist who balloons.'" And so the next day, Connie Wolf found Big Spring, Texas, on the map, and she went off and got the record. "I like a balloonist who balloons," she heard. It rang through her ears, up there in the sky, for two days, popping goofballs like Chiclets.

Abby's airplane went rumbling down the runway, and Connie waved. "Goodbye, dear!" she shouted. The airplane went into the air. "Have a safe trip!" she said with glee, and then she said, "Oh, Abby, turn on your strobe sparkler! Turn it on! You'll get lost in all this humid stuff. Oh, Abby, don't get lost!

"Poor Abby," she said, driving back across the street, home. "Poor Howard Hughes," she said. "Poor Mr. Nixon. Oh, my poor head."

Alfred Wolf died on May 29, 1985. He was 80. I went to see Mrs. Wolf a few months after the obituary appeared. It was winter. The apple trees were bare. The airplane was gone.

She took me upstairs into a room I hadn't been allowed to enter before. It was littered with boxes. Hundreds of boxes filled with thousands of newspaper clippings, awards, plaques, certificates, and all manner of honors paid to Alfred Wolf, the great American aviator, and Connie Wolf, the eccentric aviatrix. "Boxes of junk," Mrs. Wolf said, standing there. "All this junk. I don't know what to do with it." That was when she told me she was selling the house, selling Wingover, her home for more than 50 years.

"Where will you go?" I asked.

"We don't talk about that," she said. She said she wanted no obituary, that was the main thing. "I just want my cinders sprinkled over some field," she said.

She had already sold Abby's airplane. She had sold her big red farm tractor. She had given away her Mustang convertible. She had gotten rid of everything, except these stupid boxes.

It was a bitterly cold day, but it was a clear day. Connie Wolf was packing up her life with Alfred Wolf—cleaning up after all the adventures—and then she would be going, too. That was it. Abby was gone. Everything else was junk.

The material for the Liberty Bell balloon is a rip-stop nylon. Mrs. Wolf has a piece of it, and she is showing it to me again. She

just got a letter. It is signed by some members of We the People
200, the outfit organizing Philadelphia's U.S. Constitution bicentennial events. The letter talks about how the city wants to use the
Liberty Bell balloon. They don't know how they want to use it, but
they want to use it.

"I mean, look at this letter," Connie Wolf is saying. "I don't
see how I can miss this time," she says, all happy. She is happy the
way a young girl is happy receiving her first invitation to the prom.
"They're going to use it. Don't you think? Don't you think this
time it's going to work?" she asks. "I really don't see how I can
miss with this letter," she says.

"Did I tell you about the license number I got for it? 'N-200-
PA.' Isn't that wonderful? It'll be in big white letters. Did I tell you
the crack will be black? Isn't that funny? It says it in the contract:
'The crack will be black.' Ha! I knew you'd like that, dear.

"It's going to arrive soon. We're going to inflate it in the yard.
I've already gotten a huge tractor so I can cut down a big area
where I can lay this thing out. It's about 70 feet tall, you know, so
I need a big open space," she says, and she rattles on and on about
the Liberty Bell balloon.

She wants to go outside. She wants to drive me around the
grounds. We go into the barn. The old red farm tractor is indeed
gone, but a new one has replaced it. The Mustang is gone, but a
new Chevette has replaced it. We get into the car. She is still
talking about the Liberty Bell balloon. "You know, it's almost like
a Holy Grail, this thing," she says. "It would certainly amuse Abby.

"So, my dear, there's your answer," she says. "It's a Holy Grail.
And I hope it works. I hope it does this city some good."

We drive into the woods and emerge through a clearing. We
are on the runway. She stops, waits, then hits the accelerator,
hits it hard. She wants to show me just how smooth this runway is.
She is going fast. It indeed is a smooth runway. She is going

faster—this is certainly one velvety smooth runway. She is going faster and faster and faster, and it seems as though we might take off, like in *Chitty Chitty Bang Bang*. She seems to want to drive the car right into the sky. She floors it. She delights in it. She is proud of it. She is 82 years old, and she is still cutting the grass on this runway, grooming it low and smooth, even though no airplanes land here anymore.

Pinball   4

Inside the pinball factory—a low, red, boring building on the corner of California and Roscoe Avenues in North Chicago—there were birthdays happening. The people with the birthdays had dollar bills pinned to their shirts, like enormous paper brooches. You were supposed to get the hint. You were supposed to say, "Happy birthday!" and hand the person another buck. Clara Franklin, who had just turned 59, ended her day with $198 attached to her chest.

"This place has changed tremendously," she said. She is a big woman all done up in a blue lamé sweater. "New peoples come in, they got more rights than I do. But I sit back and hold my mouth."

Clara has put 18 years of her life into the pinball factory, sitting on a stool in "the 31 Department," snapping rubber bands around pegs. If you are looking to understand the essence of pinball, a game celebrating its sixtieth anniversary this year—a piece of Americana that despite all odds refuses to die—Clara Franklin is a good place to begin.

For factory work, she said, this job is decent. "It's a nice clean place; they have strict rules here lately, you know, like you can't bring any food in, the food was getting in the games and stuff, but other than that. . . ."

A bell rang. The women of the 31 Department got up—most of them were dressed up fancy, in heels, silk, lace, leather—and they went to the wash room, washed, stood by the door, and waited for the next bell to ring, signalling permission to go to the cafeteria. It was like grade school. It was a rainy Wednesday and there was a hot dog truck parked out front.

Clara got excited. "And now when they hire somebody new here, you got to bring your high school paper!" she said. "That's right! That's not only here, it's everywhere. My sister works at Bell's telephone, if you clean the john in the office, you got to have your high school paper. So you know I couldn't get no job if I ever left here. It's not like I could just quit."

So over the years Clara has held onto her job, doing what she'd been told to do, acting like a real good "workaholic," as she put it, and from a distant viewpoint it is easy to see this woman not as a person, but as a thing, rolling through this life, wrapped in lamé, all sparkles, flipped here and flipped there by the rules of her employer, family, culture, social class. In this way Clara looks, as anyone can, just like a pinball in a pinball machine.

When considering pinball's sixtieth anniversary, some people might think: So what? Who cares about pinball? Pinball is for people with tattoos. Pinball is for people who roll Marlboro boxes up in their undershirt sleeves. Or something.

The idea of pinball does not, as a rule, sit near the surface of man's consciousness. Which is precisely the point of pinball. Pinball is meaningless. Pinball is joyful, or hateful, depending on what kind of a day you're having. Pinball is pure emotion, a kind of kinetic passion occurring under glass. If you are a player, then you know all of this. You know the oneness. The nothingness. Right? Okay.

It's the nonplaying public that presently requires attention. Pinball is not something that a person can simply be told about. Pinball is like love, or God, or death. Pinball is something one discovers, alone, in a moment of self-realization. Nonplayers might want to enter the subject simply by realizing that pinball is a masterpiece of pop culture. Here is a game that has survived the trends and tastes and energies of vastly different generations. When you look at its record of survival—for decades the game was banned in major U.S. cities, and then right when the ban was lifted, video games got invented and nearly wiped pinball off the map for good—you have to wonder what this game has got.

Suddenly, in 1990, pinball is popular again. Rock stars play pinball. Pinball now accounts for 30 percent of coin-op game revenues; just five years ago that number was a measly five percent. At a coin-op industry trade show last March, I was intrigued to see the rows and rows of video games, displayed in all their high-tech fancy—all looking bored. Lonely. Jealous, perhaps. Nobody was playing them. Instead, the people were lined up five and six rows deep, waiting to get on games like The Phantom of the Opera, a new pinball by Data East, in digital stereo, and Whirlwind, by William's Electronics Games. Like most modern pinballs, Whirlwind could talk—"The storm is coming!" it shouted, "Return to your homes!"—and it also had a fan attached to the top so that when the storm finally came, you got air in your face.

Pinball is the game that won't die. Pinball taps some sweet spot in the human spirit. What is it? What is the soul of this old machine?

"I will tell you what sells a game," said Steve Kordek, a pinball designer. At 78, a Polish immigrant's son, he is short, solidly packed, and passionate about two things: the Catholic church and pinball. "What sells a pin game is—and I'm giving you some inside information here—the player looks at the game, it attracts him, it's got some goofy design on it or something, and he looks at it, and he says, 'Holy Cripe, what the hell is that?'"

Kordek works one floor above Clara at the pinball factory. Since 1937 he has witnessed the invention of the flipper, the thumper bumper, the bonus multiplier, the drop target, the electromechanical ball return, the electronic scoring system, and many other fantastic revolutionary pinball times. This is the man who had, in fact, invented multiball play. (Multiball is the Big Payoff in modern pinball; you hit all the right targets and suddenly two, three, four, sometimes five balls come at you at once. Awesome.)

In his lifetime Kordek has designed something like 600 games. "I want to get the hell out of here," he said, in one breath. And then in the next: "Oh, when I think about coming here, I get excited, uchk, I want to be here, you can understand."

A lot of people I met at the pinball factory were emotional like this.

It takes about a year, and a million dollars, and a team of about six people—from designers to programmers to graphics artists—to invent a pinball game today. Kordek's job is to head some of the design teams at WMS Industries, the parent company of Williams Electronics Games and Midway Manufacturing Company (Makers of Bally Amusement Games.) This conglomerate, which controls about 80 percent of the world's pinball manufacturing, brings out about eight new models a year. Two other pinball companies, Premier Technology (makers of Gottlieb) and Data East, manufacture the remaining 20 percent.

The style and feel of the new games have undergone a dramatic revolution in recent years. Some designers had mixed emotions about the changes. Some of them were, frankly, pissed off.

A decade ago, pinballs were difficult, mean, violent. This was the macho era for pinball, with games designed around themes of war, death, sex, sorcerers, bombs, destruction. Now you see games like Cyclone, which features a happy little amusement park, and Silver Slugger, which is about cartoon aliens playing baseball, and Taxi, which is, simply, a ride in a cab. You see pinballs which are more like toys, with gizmos attached, like Whirlwind, with the fan. Earthshaker is the first pinball game to actually shake. Elvira and the Party Monsters has little rubber boogie men that jump up and down and dance. What you see now is kinder, gentler pinball. Cute pinball. Lite Pinball.

Steve Ritchie, a designer at Williams, hates this cutesy stuff he's been expected to dream up lately. "I'm treating my player like he's a stupid jerk," said Ritchie, who prefers his early macho machines—F-14 Tomcat, Black Knight 2000, High Speed. Ritchie's goal had always been to give the player the ultimate pinball challenge. "And now I'm telling him every fucking move to make. 'Don't flip!' 'Go for the wall!' I'm pointing out every damn shot, okay? If you're a total bozo, you can play."

A lot of people at the pinball factory were intense like this. Pinball attracts soulful people.

Some say pinball had to get easier, that the whole flavor of the game had to change, if it was to survive.

"Kids today have a different mentality," said Mark Ritchie, another Williams designer (and Steve Ritchie's younger brother). "Before, the idea with pinball was to be the best, show all your friends what you could do. Today, kids want instant gratification. They want the instant thrill, okay? Back then, it was: work for the big thrill. Now it's: I want the big thrill straight up, or I'm not gonna play.

"So, yes, I'm making games easier. Yes, it bothers me

tremendously. But you can't change it. My brother wants to change the face of the industry. Let me tell you something, the industry changes your face, whether you like it or not."

The first little sign of trouble for pinball happened in 1941— when it was outlawed in some cities. This was before the flipper was invented. Pinballs in those days were mostly games of chance. You shot the ball and watched it meander down the playfield bouncing off pins, thus the name: "pin-ball." It was the chance factor that inspired the ban in Los Angeles, New York, even Chicago, pinball's birthplace and mecca. Some machines were even equipped to spit out winnings, like slot machines.

So in 1941, New York Mayor Fiorello LaGuardia put on the greatest show of pinball-bashing by actually taking a pinball machine and, with a sledge hammer, bashing it. He also dumped some machines into the East River.

Then came 1947, when the flipper was invented. Gottlieb designer Harry Mabs put six flippers onto a game called, Humpty Dumpty, and all of a sudden pinball was no longer a game of chance. It was a skill game; you could swat the ball, move it this way and that, and get good at it. Mabs's invention inspired other designers to add flippers. Six flippers. Everybody just figured flippers were things that came by the half-dozen.

Enter Steve Kordek, a young electrician, who said, in so many words, "What the hell? Why do we need these flippers all over the place?" He revolutionized the game, putting two flippers at the bottom of the playfield.

"And that's where they've been ever since," Kordek told me. "Yes. Uchk. I'm telling you it was an amazing time, very very exciting."

He told me that he had a lot of other inventions. He looked down at a clipboard. He had prepared a list. "Yes, I was the first ever to make a single drop target on a pin game," he said. "Yes, yes, yes, and I was the first to make two moving targets on a game. . . . I don't know. Don't ask me where the hell I get these crazy ideas, okay?" He didn't like being interrupted. He was on a roll. He became animated. He began to demonstrate, putting his hands up in the air, bobbing his head up, then down, then over, looking just like a pinball in a pinball machine.

"Excited?" he asked. "Good," he said.

A lot of people at the pinball factory were entertaining like this.

In some cities the ban on pinballs was not lifted until as late as 1976. Then, with the 1980s, came the video explosion. "Like an atomic bomb," said Kordek, "video took over."

Video games brought in an amazing $5 billion in 1981. "It was as if a giant fire hose had been turned on and started spraying money, okay?" recalled Pat Lawlor, designer of Whirlwind. "Video changed the entire face of this quiet little industry. And we were writing pinball's epitaph. Because here you had a game that came in a cabinet and you didn't have to do any maintenance on it. And the operators said, 'I don't ever want to see another pinball machine again.' Boom. It was over."

Pinball was faced with its final moment of truth. "Do something!" designers shouted to one another. And they did. They discovered this: Make a game easy, more accessible, and more people will play it.

Thus, the new lite games.

Add to that the fact that there was a video game crash in 1984. Volume dipped below $2.5 billion. For many reasons. First, home video brought to kids the notion that you don't have to shell out quarters for this kind of fun; mom can get you an Atari and an entire arcade's worth of cartridges for your living room. Second, video games began losing some of their allure when they became too easy for kids, too predictable. A video game is nothing but a computer program, and computer programs can be figured out, memorized.

Unlike pinball. Nobody can memorize a pinball game. In pinball, one day you're awesome, the next day you suck. Because you have moods. Because a person has influence over a pinball machine. Because a person can never gain complete mastery over, as Kordek put it, "that doggone crazy metal sphere."

Pinball is infinite.

Video games did one wonderful thing for pinball: they brought people back into arcades. People with quarters in their sweaty little palms. People who eventually grew bored with video. They looked around. And there was a pinball machine. It looked different from the old pinballs. It looked odd compared with a video game: so physical, so mechanical, so actual.

"Holy Cripe, what the hell is that?"

To answer the question, "What is the soul of this old machine," consider, finally, Python Anghelo, the factory philosopher, or the factory eccentric, or the factory weirdo, depending on whom you talk to. Python, a designer, was born in Transylvania, Romania, and he claims to have gotten his training in Europe, painting frescos in churches. "Python," people ask, "Why would you go from frescos in churches to pinballs?"

"Because pinball has more influence," he told me. He is a big man with lots of black hair which, he said, he used to wear in pigtails with bones tied to the ends. "Pinball is the new altar," he said. "I call a pinball back-glass the new stained glass of the cathedral."

Python's most notable game was the classic Pin-Bot, which featured a robot surrounded by planets; the goal was to shoot balls into the robot's eyes, at which point the robot said, "Now I see you," and shot the balls back at you. "First I wrote a poem about it, then I made it," said Python.

Human beings, Python said, are attracted to games like this on a fundamental level. "There is the fascination of man, since the beginning of time, with the sphere," he said. "We cannot control the earth, the moon, the sun, the atom, and man always wants control. Pinball is basically another sphere. And the one controlling this little sphere is us. It hits things, it goes up a ramp. That's why in my game Cyclone, I invented the first winding ramp. The ball doesn't come straight down. The ball wiggles toward you—as a reward it dances for you."

People at the pinball tend to roll their eyes when Python gets to theorizing.

But if you think of what he said, and if you picture Clara Franklin, the lady in the 31 Department who has been snapping rubber bands around pegs for the last 18 years, you begin to arrive at something.

The ultimate pinball game? Python says it would be a giant one, the size of a stadium. Instead of a ball you'd have "a giant puck with rubber sides. And you'd put your family in it, your mother-in-law, whoever. And you'd shoot this puck across this huge stadium with gigantic jet bumpers, and ramps, and water canons. You'd spray them, right? You'd be in total control of this playfield. And your poor family, you'd get even with them for all the nonsense they did to you."

Or you could put your boss in it, or the CEO of your corporation, or we could all get together and put the IRS in it. And meter maids.

Control over this enormous machine, that's what everybody

is after. Even Steve Kordek, the sage of the factory, said it: "In pinball the player's goal is control," he said. "Control of his own destiny. It's a hell of a phrase, but it's true."

Kordek's theory reminded me of one important thing Clara Franklin had said to me. "I got six years to go, and I thank God; I hope I make it," she had said. "If I left here? If I left here, I would like to have a store, a candy store. Or a church. I would like to have a mission where I could feed all the peoples that wasn't able to eat, for free, twice a week."

She had her ambitions. She wasn't just a pinball in a pinball machine. Nobody is. Pinball, I think, is one place you can go when you're feeling like one. Pinball reminds you: You are never just a thing, bouncing around in somebody else's machine. In pinball, you get to work the flippers.

The Slinky Lady   5

Betty James, 75, comes to work every morning here at the Slinky factory at the end of Beaver Street. It isn't a fancy place; no big neon signs announcing "The Home of the Slinky" or anything. There is a junkyard next door, honeysuckle invading the parking lot, and outside her office window Betty has a birdfeeder set up. Each day 36,000 original metal Slinkys are made, boxed, wrapped and shipped out of this factory to toy stores on every continent in the world except Antarctica. And that's not counting all the Slinky juniors, the plastic Slinkys, the plastic Slinky juniors, the Slinky pull toys, and the Slinky glasses with the eyeballs that pop out.

Slinky is definitely the most famous thing to ever come out of Hollidaysburg, Pennsylvania, a tiny blip of a town tucked within one deep fold of the Allegheny Mountains, where James Industries, maker of the Slinky for all of Slinky's 48 years of life, is located. Technically speaking, the first Slinky was made in Philadelphia, but Betty moved the company out here to central Pennsylvania in 1961. Betty is the one who made the Slinky what it is today, although this was not exactly what she originally set out to do with her time here on earth.

"Life is so uncertain," Betty will tell you, "at its best." There you have one of life's deceptively simple certainties with which Betty James is extremely well acquainted.

Betty stands just over five feet tall, gets her hair done once a week, dresses in dresses every day and walks with so much dignity she reminds you of Queen Elizabeth except with a more relaxed sense of humor. If you are looking to find the essence of Slinky, you really can't get any closer than by just being with Betty.

She is, after all, the one who came up with the name Slinky. Her husband, Richard James, invented the Slinky, but he's long gone by now. Richard was the love of Betty's life, but in 1960 he up and moved to Bolivia to join a religious cult. Betty has definitely seen a lot in her lifetime that no human being could ever in her wildest dreams predict.

"Oh, I have had an exciting life," says Betty, sitting behind her desk in a big olive-colored swivel chair. The walls are paneled and covered with plaques honoring Betty for things like Excellence in Packaging and Shipping Punctuality/Fill Rate. These plaques are interspersed among pictures of Betty's six children and 16 grandchildren. Betty raised her kids without Richard, just as she raised the Slinky without Richard.

Just one set of double doors away from Betty's office are the whir, clank, cha-ching and other industrial music put out by the six Slinky machines in action. These are the exact same machines that always made Slinkys, and Number One, as it is called, is still notoriously slow. There are barrels of water under the Slinky machines, each stenciled with a request: "No Spitting In Barrels." One hundred twenty people work around the clock in shifts making Slinky after Slinky after Slinky, plus the lesser items Betty has acquired over the years—pinwheels, pickup sticks,

I'm A Cheerleader pompoms and Moli Q's play shapes.

This is a quirky place. It is odd, first of all, to even find a toy still being made in the United States. Something like 150,000 items can be found on the shelves of America's toy stores on any given day, and a full 75 percent of them are imported. Toy manufacturing is extremely labor-intensive, and most American toys long ago headed offshore in search of cheap labor. But not Slinky. Another strange thing is that the Slinky company remained so small. You'll find no R&D department here at James Industries, no PR office and not a single MBA walking these halls. You want a Slinky press kit? There isn't one. But Betty will happily let you see a scrapbook with some brittle newspaper clippings from the 1950s in it. If you'd like you can even use the photocopier.

"We're not big time," says Betty. "We like it the way it is. Slinky is like a child, and you don't exploit your child."

People with advanced degrees and calculators in their pockets become utterly dumbfounded when they hear that Betty James didn't sell Slinky to some giant toy conglomerate years ago. Wouldn't that, after all, be the American way? Betty could sign a few papers, make zillions, and go sit poolside at some lovely condo off the coast of Florida for the rest of her life instead of coming in here to this old factory five days a week. It's not as if she hasn't had offers. "Oh, I have been wooed by some of the best," says Betty, pointing out that once a week someone will breeze through here and try to buy her out. But Betty just says no, no, a thousand times no.

The closest she ever got was when CBS, the TV network, was into toys and put in a bid for Slinky. "They were offering me, you know, everything," says Betty. "And I almost did it. I went to a meeting up in their tower, in their dining room, the executive dining room, you know, real classy, and they said, 'Well, you ought to go down to our showroom and look our toys over.' So I went down, I looked, and then I called the man with whom I had been working. I said, 'I'm not going to sell to you.' And he said, 'What's the matter?' And I said, 'I don't like your toys.' I said, 'I think they look cheap. And I don't want to put my toy in there with yours.'

"It was like one of your children. You're putting it up for adoption and you don't like the family so you don't let it go."

Betty James is definitely not what you'd call a business tycoon. People might say she lets her heart make too many of her decisions. People might, for instance, wonder why Betty still makes the Slinky the same size as the original, with the same fine American steel; she could have used cheaper steel, or made it smaller, and, really, who would notice? Also, people wonder why in tarnation Betty doesn't raise prices. When Slinky first came out it retailed for $1. Now, nearly a half-century later, you can still get one for about $1.89. People say that's a pretty pathetic rate of inflation.

"No, we haven't done too badly by the public," admits Betty. "I think a lot of people think, hey, everyone else is increasing prices, we'll increase prices too. But no, I don't go by that. See, my theory is, if it's a child's toy, make it affordable. That's just what I go by."

Betty defies the conventional wisdom of just about anybody you'll talk to in the business world. Betty goes her own way. But this is nothing new. Betty will tell you her whole life she has felt like an island, just one person out here all alone trying to survive in a crazy world. Well, she was an orphan so that might have something to do with it. Her mother died when she was eight and that's when her father took off.

You'd think she'd be bitter, given some of the nasty twists of fate life has thrown her way. But Betty will just sit back, shake her head and grin, as if she is privy to some God-given insider's tip about human nature. Betty embodies the spirit of the Slinky, rolling through life according to the way life, like gravity, pushes and pulls. She learned long ago to give up the notion of control. Betty's life story is completely intertwined with Slinky's life story, and that is why the two are so much alike they could be sisters, although Betty insists it's more a mother-daughter type thing.

The essence of Slinky lies somewhere in its ordinariness. Slinky is not pretentious. This gives it a dignified quality that attracts people.

"Everyone," said the old TV commercial, "loves the Slinky. You ought to have a Slinky." That direct little jingle was written in 1961 and it's still being used today, although modified somewhat. In the 1970s they took out the xylophone and added guitar.

The truth is that everyone probably does love the Slinky. Slinky has an 87 percent recognition rate among the public. Slinky is a toy for regular people. You don't have to be smart, athletic, rich or clever to appreciate Slinky. Slinky is a toy that does not discriminate. Boys love Slinkys just like girls love Slinkys just like men love Slinkys just like women do. Slinky is universal. You pick up a Slinky and the metal feels cold against your hands. Instinctively, you know to part those coils into two halves and rock the Slinky back and forth. This is just a human drive we all have. What happens next is a completely individualized experience. Maybe you are the visual type and you become transfixed by the sight of the Slinky undulations, the geometric designs formed by a coil in motion. Maybe you are more the musical type and you like to listen to the ping-ping percussion of metal landing on metal, the dim echo of Slinky in song. Maybe you are the engineer type so you will push Slinky to its physical limits trying to see how far apart you can put your hands and still keep the Slinky in motion. Maybe you are the imaginative type and you will look at the Slinky going back and forth and you will see stories.

No matter what type you are, you will, of course, one day be faced with the problem of a tangled Slinky; one coil will bend and you will try everything in your power to bend it back perfectly but you will fail. This is a fundamental Slinky truth. Slinkys don't recuperate. A sick Slinky is a dead Slinky. When your Slinky dies you will feel totally lost for a brief period of time but then you will snap out of it. But all of this is just if you are an ordinary person.

Extraordinary people have found other uses for Slinky. A fellow in Tuscumbia, Alabama invented The Better Pecan Picker, out of a Slinky. "No more sore hands! No more sore back! Just roll it around and watch it pick up all the pecans with the greatest of ease." A lady in Maine buys thousands of Slinkys a year to use in her drapery business. Slinky is in the Smithsonian Institution as a piece of genuine Americana. Slinky was taken on the space shuttle Discovery to see if it would slink in zero gravity. After much experimentation, astronauts Rhea Seddon and Jeffrey Hoffman found out that Slinky in space was a total dud.

Physicists have long been fascinated with Slinky's usefulness in demonstrating the physics of waves. One journal article points out that "the speed of propagation of expansion waves (c), with respect to the coils of the unextended Slinky, is described by the formula $c = (kl/M) 1/2$"—in case you're interested. For further reading, try "The Slinky as a Model for Transverse Waves in a Tenuous Plasma," "Slinky Oscillations and the Notion of Effective Mass," "On Slinky: The Dynamics of a Loose, Heavy Spring," and the ever popular "Slinky Zum 40 Geburtstag—Das Spizzichino-Problem."

As you have probably guessed by now, Slinky is also popular with biologists in demonstrating the primary structure of poly-peptides.

Betty James doesn't understand too much about polypep-tides—or pecan pickers, for that matter. And, anyway, today she has more pressing concerns.

"Where shall we sit?" says Betty. Space is such a problem here at the Slinky factory. Sometimes it seems you don't have room to turn around. The insurance people have come for a meeting and Betty has given her office over to them. Well, that was better than having to sit in on the boring meeting. "Let's go to the lunchroom," Betty says. Pushing open the doors to the factory, turning right and, settling in near the candy machine, she tells the story of how Slinky came to be.

It began as the perfect American Dream:

Betty Mattas met Richard James at Penn State, where both attended college. He was a handsome and brilliant engineer, Class of 1939. They fell madly in love, got married and moved to Philadelphia, where Richard worked as an engineer at the Cramp shipyard for $50 a week. One of his jobs was to test the horsepower on the mighty naval battleships. To do this, he would use a torsion meter, and a torsion meter required the use of a torsion spring.

One day, Richard saw one one of these springs fall off his desk. It rolled over itself in the most fascinating way. He brought it home to Betty and said, "I think I can make a toy out of this."

Betty recalls: "And he said, 'We have to name this toy.' Well, I didn't know anything about toys. I really didn't. But he said find a name for it. So I was thinking and I couldn't think of anything. So I got the dictionary and I said, 'I'll try to find a word that depicts the slithering action of it.' So that's how slinky came. It just seemed to depict everything."

Slinky didn't sell at first. "A Slinky just sitting there on a shelf isn't awfully inspiring if you think about it," says Betty. "It's kind of like a blob."

Then the Gimbels department store gave Richard and Betty the use of a counter where they could demonstrate the Slinky. This was in 1945. "And it was a terrible night," recalls Betty. "It was snowing and raining, oh, it was horrible. So my husband, we had 400 Slinkys made, so he took them in and I said to him, 'Now you go ahead and I'll come in, I'll get a friend of mine, and if nobody's buying we'll come over and buy some Slinkys.' To stimulate people, you know. We thought we would have to get some enthusiasm going.

"So we got off the elevator and I can see it now, I'm looking around the toy department and I didn't see anybody, but over in one corner there's this mob of people, people everywhere, and they all had dollars in their hands, and it was, Wow! Go for it! So we went over, I didn't even have to spend my dollar. We sold 400 Slinkys in 90 minutes. And that's how we started."

Richard and Betty went on to make Slinkys out of a factory on Portico Street in Germantown. Richard would bring the Slinkys home and Betty would wrap the Slinkys with yellow paper, roll them and fold the ends in. "That was what we called packaging," Betty will tell you now. Oh, Betty laughs about some of those old days. Soon they were opening a new, larger factory in Clifton Heights with 20 employees. By 1951 they had moved the company to an even larger factory in Paoli.

Richard and Betty were happy. In particular, Betty was happy having babies. That was the main thing. Betty had what she had always dreamed of as an orphaned child: a family. And Richard was happy being rich and famous. Maybe too happy. Betty didn't like what was happening to him.

"The man I married was a delight," says Betty. "He really was. But he didn't handle success well. I don't think. The way I look at it he didn't handle it well.

"Money corrupted him," says Betty. "And power. And publicity. He liked it all. It came too fast. It was overwhelming. That's what happened. He got real important way too suddenly. And that's when he got religious."

And that's when Betty's life fell to pieces.

"These people from England, that was his first step into it," she says. "They were parasites. I don't know how he met them. They came to the house and settled in. That was horrible. That was the introduction, and that just dissolved everything. And then he announced one night, he called my son Tom and my daughter Libby and I to the downstairs and he said, 'I'm going to leave. I'm going to South America. Do you want to run the company or sell it?' And I said, 'I'll run it.'"

And Richard left. He moved to Cochabamba, Bolivia, to be a part of a religious cult that to this day Betty knows almost nothing about. "I don't even know what they believed in," says Betty. "They were perfect. And I was not. That's all I knew."

Richard wrote to her a lot at first. "He kept writing and writing and telling me that I was damned and I should come join him in South America and he was the head of the family and I should do what he said. He wanted me to join the cult and leave the children here. And he said if I didn't I was going to hell."

"And so I stayed here and sinned, I guess."

Betty soon learned that Richard had donated an awful big hunk of the family fortune to that cult. And he had been ignoring the business. "We were really for all practical purposes bankrupt," says Betty. "But I was too dumb to know it." And Betty knew nothing about business, much less anything about bringing a bankrupt business back to life, much less about how a woman survives in a man's world. And Betty had a broken heart to mend. And Betty had a whole huge lump of philosophical and spiritual madness to sort through, not to mention six kids to raise.

"I had to do something to take care of my family," says Betty. "I had to make the company work. I just had to. But it was stupid. If I had known what I was getting into I wouldn't have tried. I would not have.

"Fools walk in where angels fear to tread, you know. That is so true."

Now look what is happening. The first shift is coming in with their lunch pails and Big Gulp sodas and it looks as if Betty will have to relocate once again. "That's my only real problem here at the factory is space," Betty reasserts. She's taken to moving trailers into the parking lot and using them to hold the Slinky inventory. At this point there are so many trailers out there that the neighbors down Beaver Street seriously wonder if Betty hasn't gotten into the trailer business.

Space wouldn't be a problem if Betty could just build on the rest of the land she owns behind the factory. But the government has stepped in and declared this land part of a wetlands zone and so Betty is stuck. "It's kind of ridiculous," says Betty, standing now out on the loading dock. She looks down. The land in question is a narrow strip that separates her factory from a Conrail line. "I mean, no self-respecting animal would even come back here."

But Betty is not one to complain. Betty has no illusions. Betty knows life is full of problems and chaos. Here is how she got out of the mess Richard left her with:

The first thing she did was protect the children. She bought a big, old, empty house in Hollidaysburg where she had, at least, some aunts and uncles who might help out. She fixed the house up and had the children's bedrooms all done up exactly to match their bedrooms in the old house, right down to every piece of furniture and every stuffed animal. "The children had had enough trauma," says Betty. She remembers crying every single Sunday night for a year when she would have to leave those children. She'd get in the car and make the four-hour trek to Philadelphia, where she would stay through Thursday trying to revive the Slinky factory there. It seemed so hopeless. Richard had left her with a stack of unpaid bills sky high. She became determined to pay those bills.

A short time later, she rented a factory in Bellwood, near

Hollidaysburg, a building so small she also needed a barn and a garage for storage. Four years later, the Slinky company finally made some money. And Betty not only paid every bill, but she included a thank you note with each.

"Any one person could have said, 'Pay me now,'" says Betty. "And I would have been finished. And they didn't. They waited. And I was so thankful so I told them so."

With the company springing back, Betty needed her own factory. But she had no land. The townspeople of Hollidaysburg came to the rescue. They wanted the factory. They needed jobs. A local pharmacist and town father called Betty and said, "Meet me tomorrow morning down by the Conrail line on Beaver Street." She went. He said, "How much do you need?"

"Well," Betty recalls, "I didn't know an acre from a half acre, I mean I had no conception. So I looked and I said, 'Well, I have six kids, how about six acres?' And he said, 'Fine. Will a dollar be too much?' And I handed him a dollar."

James Industries is still a private company and does not release sales figures, but the Standard & Poor's Registry shows an estimate of $5 million to $10 million.

"See," says Betty, "I was fortunate. I wasn't clever. I was just lucky. I mean really and truly. Cleverness didn't enter into it. It was all a lot of dumb luck."

Betty takes almost no credit for turning the Slinky company around. She says it was the people who helped her that did it, her creditors, the townspeople and most notably her controller, Bob Lestochi, whom she hired 32 years ago. He took it as a temporary job. He is still with the company today. Bob knows that if Betty sells the Slinky company to some toy industry giant, he'll probably be out of a job, a pension, a future. And Betty knows this, too.

Betty's sense of loyalty to her workers and to the town is what keeps the Slinky out here in the middle of, relatively speaking, nowhere.

"Over the years I could have just sold it, and I would have been better off, much better off," she admits. "But you know, these people that are here working, some of them have been with me, oh, I think the average is probably around 20 years. And a lot of them for 25, 28 years. Well, you can't turn your back on that. They're good people. And we're their livelihood. You know, and I have to think of them. And I do think of them. Because I like them. Not all of them, you know, but most of them.

"And I don't care for greed," says Betty. "I have everything I need. Me and my dogs. Oh, you'll die—their names are Mork and Mindy, isn't that original? You know, I had heard of that TV show, but I had never even seen it. It was just one of those things.

"So, I am happy. I live alone in the big house I raised my kids in. People say, 'Why do you live there alone?' It is a big place, you know. But I say, 'It's home.'"

Betty's feelings for her home run especially deep considering the fact that the whole place burned down in 1974. She mentions this fact as if she were referring to a day of grocery shopping. "Oh, yes, the house was completely gutted. I was out of it for 11 months, living in a hotel. I had it all done over again." She put it back exactly as it was before, same layout, same wall coverings, same furniture in the children's rooms.

Just another one of life's little bowling balls that rolled over Betty. Betty doesn't understand why in the world she should be angry at life for asking her to participate in this sort of sport.

"You know, you fall and you land on your feet," she says. "You hope you do." And you don't count on standing up for very long. Because life, as Betty says, is, at its best, uncertain. Happy people, she says, are people who embrace that notion, people who surrender control. Happy people, she says, are people who stop being gluttonous with the world's riches and stop feeling all big and entitled. Happy people are people who focus on what's important: other people. In fact, that might be the secret to happiness in old age right there. "Being loving," Betty says. "And being loved. I think. I can't think of anything else that is more important. Being content. That's it. Just being satisfied with your lot. You're not envious. You're not greedy. You don't want the unattainable. You're not striving to prove something.

"People now think they deserve some individual flattery. You know, 'I am wonderful, I have done this, I am doing my own thing.' I think so, don't you? I think people are greedier, or they're more just out for themselves. I think everyone's afraid that they're going to give up something for somebody else. And you know the funny thing is, if people would just know how much pleasure they would get out of just giving something up for somebody else. Not always. But I mean basically."

In the end, Betty gets her office back. Tom, her oldest son and sales manager, tells her the insurance meeting was just as thrilling as always. Tom, a Shakespeare scholar, is keeping the tradition of his mother's soul intact in this place. The rest of Betty's children are off doing other things, and the family remains very close.

Richard James died 19 years ago in Bolivia, and no one knows how.

The essence of Slinky is in its history. Slinky is resilient. Slinky is a survivor. Slinky is loyal. Slinky is honest. Slinky never got a big head. Slinky never had to do anything tricky to win hearts. Slinky just is Slinky. The thing about being ordinary is that there is so much dignity in it.

The Pet Shrink | 6

As a dog trainer of some note—indeed, as the grand pooh-bah of canine psychotherapy—Richard Kelly would like nothing more than to get his face on the cover of a magazine. "I mean, wouldn't that make a cover story, a guy in a wheelchair training dogs?" he says in the car. Bill Barry says, yeah, it would. Richard, 37, has been in the wheelchair for about three years now. Bill is his partner. Richard is a very heavy man, weighing well over 300 pounds. It makes life difficult. Bill, 33, is skinny and spry, just under 120, you'd guess. They care about each other. Together they went to a tanning salon yesterday, so that when the reporter came, they would look good.

"K-9 Heroes" is the name of their dog training company near Washington, D.C. and Richard Kelly is the brains behind it. What he offers is in-home, personalized dog training, and what he guarantees is this: "Within two and a half hours, we'll turn your dog into the perfect lady or gentleman of the house." It makes no matter how old your dog is. It makes no matter what kind of dog you have. It's true. In just one afternoon, you could see your dog stop all that annoying chewing, stop that excessive barking, stop drooling all over the linoleum whenever you and your loved ones sit down to dine.

Richard Kelly has a secret—something, he says, that nobody but he and Bill know. They never strike the dog. Never hurt it. "We don't change its personality. We don't turn it into a zombie. We never break its spirit," Richard promises. And it works. People are amazed. Their mouths drop. The miracle happens to about 750 dogs a year in and around Washington.

Interestingly, Richard Kelly's clients almost never see Richard Kelly. At least not anymore. He doesn't get out much. To most people, Richard Kelly is just a voice over the telephone, making promises. And when people hire him, Bill shows up. The people ask about Richard. The people want to meet Richard. "Where's Richard?"

Today, for the first time in three years, Richard Kelly will himself appear.

"Do I look tan?" he asks in the car.

"Not really," Bill says. They are headed for Humphrey's house. Humphrey is a frenzied black labrador retriever in need of some heavy-duty behavior modification.

"Where's my knife?" Richard asks.

"Right here," Bill says, handing him one with a long, shiny, serrated blade. The knife is for Richard to scratch his ankles with. His ankles itch because he has hives on them because he ate clam chowder yesterday and the milk in it made him break out. He can't reach his ankles because his middle is too bulky to bend. So he uses the knife. The tanning salon adventure yesterday was Richard's first time out of the house in six months. He has a lot of problems. Bill helps Richard. He'll put Richard to bed. He'll empty Richard's urine bottle. He'll pull Richard's pants up when they sag below his belly and get bunched up underneath him. He'll stop at the drugstore for him and get pain pills, itch ointment, allergy medicine, sunburn pain relief.

"What do you think are the chances of me getting on the cover of that magazine?" Richard asks.

"I don't know," Bill says.

The other question, of course, is: how does it happen? how does a man end up being a controller of dogs?

Two things about his business Richard Kelly refuses to reveal publicly: How much his service costs ("People freak.") and the secret behind his magic. A person would have to call him first and listen to his pitch. But beware. Richard is a whiz at telephone sales. Give him your ear, and he will have you signing a contract. So good is Richard at selling his service that Bill, working seven days a week from noon to midnight, has not had a day off in more than a year.

Bill says he likes the work. It can be rewarding. He did a good job on a dalmatian the other day. The dog's name was Apollo, and he belonged to Laurie Costello, a young woman who was a beauty queen in a former life. There was a picture of Laurie on the counter in which Laurie was smiling wide, wearing a sparkling dress, holding an enormous trophy. Her dog meant a lot to her. Apollo had the body of a thoroughbred—and the mind of a juvenile delinquent. Laurie wanted him to act right, and Bill was helping her, but then Laurie's mother walked in.

"I don't want nothing more to do with that dog," the mother hollered, all excited. "My nerves are shot, just shot." She was just getting back from the pool. "Do you want to see what he did to me?" she said, pulling down the strap of her bathing suit and revealing her right breast. Bill looked at it. There were big purple bruises on it. And on her arm, and on her thigh. "Pulled me down the sidewalk. I went flying. I couldn't do nothing!" Apollo kept pulling and pulling, and apparently he would have kept on pulling, forever and ever, had he not gotten the leash—and Laurie's mother—wrapped around a stump. "And no one will believe me."

"No-I-did-not-say-I-don't-believe-you," Laurie put in.

"My God! What do I have to do to get someone to notice me around here? Throw myself out the window?" the mother said. The father came in then and looked at everybody. He looked at Apollo. "He chews," he said. "My feeling is, you give a dog the run of the house, and he'll chew. You'd do it, too, if you were left alone all the time when you were little." He put a fruit bowl out. It had a big pineapple sticking out of the middle of it. He took the sports page into the bedroom.

"All the time he holds it down!" the mother said. She was talking about Apollo's head. "Like a hound dog! And I keep saying, 'Apollo, get your head up! Walk like a show dog!'" Bill nodded politely. In front of Laurie's beauty pageant picture, on the counter, sat two tiny ceramic dogs, dalmatians, positioned just so. They were looking up at the beauty queen, as if in awe. "Arf! Arf!"

"And I say, 'Apollo, get your head up!'" the mother went on. "'You are not a hound dog. You-are-a-show-dog!'"

Later Bill said, "You see a lot in this line of work. Most of the time the problem isn't with the dog. The problem is with the people." In other words, a dog has a reason for wanting to wrap a woman around a stump.

Another day, another dog. Richard and Bill are headed for Humphrey's. Bill's looking quite dapper today, dressed in a blue sport coat and a white cap. The tanning salon yesterday gave him a golden tan. Richard, on the other hand, got scorched. Bad things always seem to happen to Richard. Richard served in Vietnam. He can't talk about it, not even to Bill. Ceiling fans freak him out. He says he had a terrible childhood. He had very bad dreams. He ran away, nearly became a ward of the state, got sent to military school, got married, but that didn't work out, and then to top everything else off, he ate that clam chowder yesterday. In the car, he reaches for his ankle with the knife. It makes his shoulder hurt. And, of course, his hips. "Oh, Billy, the pain. It's never been this bad," he says.

"Give me one of my pills. God bless you, Billy, God bless you." In the back of the car is a cooler filled with beer for Richard and Perrier for Bill. Richard says he drinks a case of beer a day.

"And no one will believe me," he says. Bill says it's true. Bill says Richard never gets drunk, though. Bill says Richard should donate his liver to science.

So that is the situation as the K-9 Heroes pull up to Humphrey's house. Kevin and Joy Keller are the owners. "We've been so looking forward to this," Joy says, and then Richard eases out of the car. Bill gets him in the wheelchair. Richard is wearing a Hawaiian-print shirt and gold-mirrored sunglasses, and he is indeed very big. His neck is wider than his head. He lights a cigarette and leaves it hanging out of his mouth.

"Hi," he says.

The people look at him. The people look at this, the grand pooh-bah of canine psychotherapy. Humphrey is in the backyard, barking.

Richard Kelly says he has always had dogs on his mind, has always dreamed about dogs, ever since the tender age of five, when it happened. It happened in the neighbor's yard.

He got attacked by a poodle.

The event was internalized, interpreted and reinterpreted

and finally made metaphorical, shaping a young boy's view of the world.

"The poodle bit me on the tush," he explains. He had to get rabies shots. "Ten-inch syringes, 21 of them, right through the abdomen." From that point on, he says, he started having nightmares. The same dream, every time. "It was about that poodle. It would be a beautiful day outside, a beautiful afternoon. The fathers would be out playing with the sons, and they're all cooking on the grill and playing badminton," he says. "All the fathers with the sons. And all of a sudden, the air raid sirens go off. Everything changes! Everybody starts scrambling for their houses. The sky is darkening! Everything is pitch black! And then, all the people are safe in their houses with the doors and windows locked. Except me. The only thing that's out there is the street lights and me. And then, from around the corner, comes . . . Goo Goo!"

Goo Goo, the giant poodle. Goo Goo could talk. Goo Goo could walk upright. Goo Goo would come after Richard. Goo Goo would gobble Richard up. "And it would be the same sensation, when he ate me up, the same pain that I felt from those needles." Richard had this nightmare a lot. "Every single night, I swear to you, sometimes twice a night, every single night for eight years. The same exact nightmare. Same block. Same dog. Same bright, beautiful day. The fathers and the sons. The same sirens. The sky would go black."

Then he turned 13. "And one night I killed the dog in my dream. And I never had the dream again. True story. I swear. The point is, I've been getting even with the dogs ever since."

It wasn't too long after he killed off Goo Goo that Richard Kelly ran away from home. He says he just couldn't take it anymore. He talks of revenge—of a life dedicated to getting even with dogs—and yet he really has no interest in hurting dogs.

To understand what Richard Kelly does to dogs, to understand his magic, you first have to understand that a lot of dogs are a lot like Humphrey, Kevin and Joy's frenzied black lab. A lot of dogs go through life nervous, anxious, unruly, frantic. People yell at them because they are this way, and, of course, they are this way because people yell at them. "Get down! Get up! Get out of here! Get in here! Hold your head up, you mangy mutt, you-are-a-show-dog!" The dog doesn't know what's going on. He lives in a constant state of confusion, a kind of frozen adolescence. "What did I do now?" "Eeek!" "Leave me alone!" "Help!"

The problem is borders, and Richard Kelly's magic, his message to the world, is all about borders.

Kevin and Joy take notes while Richard sits in their living room, lecturing. He begins losing his voice—laryngitis is an occasional problem—and so Bill fills in every now and again. Humphrey is still in the backyard, barking. A parakeet with a big blue belly is in a cage, chirping. The bird goes back and forth on his perch, back and forth, in an odd liquid motion, as if break-dancing. The lecture goes on. Bill is quick to put the ashtray under Richard's cigarette because Richard can't see it; his neck, like his middle, is just too bulky to bend. Bill looks like a skeleton in comparison; it looks as if all of Bill's flesh came off one day and somehow ended up on Richard.

"You're doing fine, just fine," Bill assures Richard, who stops talking, saying he's rusty, he hasn't done this in three years. Kevin and Joy don't seem too sure about any of this. Humphrey keeps barking. The bird keeps chirping. Bill demonstrates the proper way to use the word "no." "It's gotta be loud, sharp, crisp, curt and mean—like a punch," he says.

As instructed, Kevin and Joy stand up, one by one, and practice this—"No!" "No!" "No!"—and lo and behold, the bird stops chirping. No one seems to notice. "No!" "No!" "No!" The bird stops break-dancing. "No!" "No!" "No!" The bird goes to the bottom of the cage and sinks his neck in. "What'd I do?"

Richard learned his dog-training techniques back in the 1970s and has been perfecting them ever since, and teaching them to Bill. Again, it is a simple matter of borders. Richard learned that if you draw a line—if you give a dog a very clear, firm set of rules—and tell a dog that he's not allowed to go over that line for any reason, ever, and if you are consistent, your dog will calm down and like you better. He won't be confused. He'll know that as long as he stays inside these borders, life will be fine; inside these borders is a place of peace. Inside these borders he is free. It isn't a hard lesson. It takes a dog about half an hour to get it.

"No!" "No!" "No!"

The way of delivering the "No," plus essential pauses, plus negative stimulus, plus praise, is the secret to Richard's success. He has a way of doing it that a dog picks up quick. Timing is crucial.

If it takes a dog just half an hour to get it, then how come Richard allots two and a half hours for his miracle cure? A few reasons. First, he wants people to think they're getting their money's worth. Second, he has to teach people a lot about dog psychology, because the key to an obedient dog is an informed owner. Finally, what it takes a dog half an hour to learn, it takes people a lot longer to learn. People have other issues. People get mixed up about borders. People are always looking for freedom on the outside, feeling fenced in. Dogs get fenced in, and they feel free. No wonder people are so much crazier than dogs.

Bill says it's ironic. Richard, the teacher, is the one person who never learns the lesson. "It's like the clam chowder," says Bill. "He knew he would get hives if he ate it. But it's like he always weighs the desire for something over the punishment, and the desire always wins. He'll say, 'Well, the hives are worth it.'" And it's like his wheelchair. Richard says his problem is hip dysplasia. He says he could walk okay a few years ago.

The doctors said he needed some operations. He didn't get them. He sat home. He ate a lot of food. He drank a lot of beer. He gained weight, so much weight that pretty soon his hips couldn't hold him up anymore. He found a wheelchair in a catalog, ordered it and sat in it. He gained more weight. Bill says the situation is getting bad. Bill says maybe Richard is killing himself. Bill's thinking of putting Richard on a fish diet. Bill's thinking of telling Jimmy, the guy who brings the beer, to bring light beer next time.

"No!" "No!" "No!" Bill will say, and he'll deliver it like a punch—loud, sharp, crisp, curt and mean—but his timing, in this case, will be off.

Kevin and Joy are thoroughly pleased with the miracle bestowed upon Humphrey, who, in just two and a half hours, is indeed a calm, contented dream dog by their side.

"You delivered! You delivered!" they keep saying to Richard. "I just can't believe this," Joy says. "I need a Valium," Kevin says. They sign a contract to put Humphrey through the deluxe course. Most people do this. In just six more hours, the K-9 Heroes can have your dog obeying your every command—"Sit!" "Lie Down!" "Heel!"—off-leash, 100 feet from you, with distractions built in and without your actually uttering a word. And it works. People are amazed. Their mouths drop.

Bill gives Humphrey a pat on the head, gets Richard in the car, and the K-9 Heroes drive away. "Ohhh. Wheeew. Ahhh. Wheeww," Richard says, breathing hard. His hips are really hurting. His ankles are really itching. "Get me one of them Benadryls, Bill. Do I have hives on my back? Whew! God bless you, Billy. I don't know what I'd do without you, Billy. God bless you. Turn on the air conditioner."

They pull into a shopping center. "Now, Bill, I want you to get something medicated. Tell the pharmacist, tell him what's happened to my legs and that I'm going out of my mind."

"All right."

"Oh, and Bill, what do you think I should use instead of that knife on my legs? Should I use, like, a hair brush or something?"

"I don't think you should scratch. It just makes it worse."

"Okay, yeah, okay. Billy, do I look tan?"

"Not really."

In the end, Richard and Bill make one complete journey around the Beltway, training dogs. Dinner doesn't come until midnight. Richard orders himself three appetizers, three entrees and five double shots of tequila.

He talks to me, finally. I've been in the back seat all day, with the Perrier and the beer and a brown bag with Richard's Benadryl and urine bottle in it. It is good to get out. "You know, I would give anything to get on the cover of that magazine," Richard says. It is, after all, the reason he has taken himself out of the house today. "To show my dad. See, I can't talk to him. There's a rift. So, this way, you know, he'll find out how I'm doing. You know, him thinking I would never be a success. Look at me! No other dog trainer can charge as much as me!"

The food arrives. The waitress—the tattoo on her arm reads "Trouble Maker"—has to pull over another table to fit all of the plates. Richard looks at his food. There is a lot of it. He looks at Bill's food—a lobster. He doesn't want his own food. He wants Bill's food.

"You have your own lobster," Bill says.

"Yours is better."

"It's the same lobster!"

"Nope, you got a better one. Just one taste of it, Billy, please?"

For the first time today, Bill puts his foot down. He refuses to give Richard any of his lobster and resolves to have every uneaten bit of it wrapped up to go. Richard has his food wrapped up, too. They roll out with three shopping bags full of food.

Richard is zonked, spent. He talks about getting his picture on the cover of a magazine. Or how about a book? How about a TV movie of the week? He talks about whips. Baseball bats. "And I was just a little kid." He talks about the air raid sirens. The fathers locking all the doors. The sky going black.

"See, I could get, probably, a picture of me sitting in a wheelchair and as many dogs as you want. What do you want—50? 100? All kinds of dogs just lying down on the ground, some sitting all around me. Which would be quite a unique picture, you know? Yeah, it would be some unique picture. It's something I'd really be proud of. It's something my dad would see." Hucktooo. He spits out the window. He groans. He moans. It's late. Everything hurts.

Bill gets Richard into the house. Richard complains, saying why isn't Billy a better friend, a more patient friend?

The next morning, Bill sleeps in. He nearly forgets that it is Father's Day. He gives his dad the leftover lobster, then heads over to Richard's.

A
Groundhog 7

Once I had a groundhog in my life. I think of him from time to time. You can learn so much from a groundhog.

What happened was the guy next door came over and said I should step outside. He said: "I don't know how to tell you this." He said: "You have a rat living in your yard that is so big, let me put it this way—even your cats are afraid of it."

I looked at him. "It's not a rat," I said. "It's a groundhog."

(You should always defend your friend's reputation.)

But I was busted. The groundhog had been living under my shed for some time.

I didn't mind the groundhog. It was autumn, and the animal had come for the apples that were falling like bombs off the tree. I would get up in the morning and find him outside my kitchen window, sitting on his hind legs, joyfully gnawing.

"How are you, groundhog?" I would mumble, half asleep.

The groundhog wouldn't answer.

(You should never try to force your friend to talk.)

Well, my neighbor thought a groundhog was worse than a rat. I said, no way. I said this groundhog was more sanitary than many of my past boyfriends. Come to think of it, this groundhog looked like many of my past boyfriends. Kind of hairy and pug-nosed. At least in my memory.

(You should not project past relationships onto present ones. But this takes practice.)

My neighbor said we would certainly have to call the health department about this. He left shaking his head with worry. Next thing I knew, his 13-year-old son was over. "A groundhog!" the boy, Danny, said. "Wow! Shouldn't we call the zoo?"

The zoo! It went on like this. One by one the neighbors would arrive and say all manner of amazingly stupid City Folk things about the groundhog living under my shed. We became hot gossip.

(When your friend is a foreigner, people will talk.)

Winter came and the groundhog went to sleep under the shed, and so, for a while, everybody shut up about us. Besides, they got all worked up about the pink van that was parked half on the sidewalk.

But I didn't forget about the groundhog. It's hard to just block a rodent out of your life; rodents teach you lessons and prepare you for the next rodent. This is the school of relationships that we women often imagine ourselves in.

Spring came and the groundhog woke up. I was planting petunias, snapdragons and stately rows of zinnias. And there, finally, was the groundhog. "Dude!" I said, spotting him. "How was your sleep?" My cats likewise tipped their hats. The family was intact and life was good.

But what happened was the groundhog ate my zinnias. And my petunias. The groundhog ate every single flower in my yard, all in one sitting, as if this was just the first course I was serving.

"YOU PIG!" I shouted at the groundhog. I went after him with the hose. "YOU WALRUS!" I shouted, not sure what name would most offend a groundhog.

(When you and your friend have your first fight, you will just swing and swing and you will have no idea where your punches will land.)

The groundhog scurried under the shed. I got on my knees, looked in, aimed the hose. Two, four, six, there were a lot of eyeballs peering back at me. There were eight, ten eyeballs in there!

My groundhog, it turned out, had a wife. My groundhog had three children. I felt betrayed. Every groundhog, just like every hairy, pug-nosed boyfriend, is the same, I thought. Lying, cheating, scumball rodent, I thought. I had given him a place to live, protected him, and what did I get? He moved the family in and was eating me out of yard and garden.

(When you are in a relationship, you think you both are seeing the world the exact same way, but you rarely are.)

Where I saw flowers, the groundhog saw: breakfast. Where I saw backstabbing, double-crossing, double-dealing disloyalty, the groundhog saw: breakfast.

It was a perceptual thing. You couldn't really blame the groundhog. But still.

We couldn't reconcile. I called Critter Control. I hated having the big yellow Critter Control truck out there where all the neighbors could see.

(When you are ending a relationship, you don't want the world to know.)

I had to go out of town suddenly. I put Danny in charge of the traps. Check these every day, I said. Call Critter Control if a groundhog is caught. The responsibility made the boy's chest swell.

I came home and the entire groundhog family had been removed. Danny came over, gave me the detailed account of the prisoners, and then presented a video. "I thought you'd want this," he said. It was a 50-minute video. Ten minutes of each trapped groundhog.

(When a relationship ends, you will want to rewind and fast forward through the details a million and 20 times.)

I took the video. I didn't know where to put it. I thought about a friend who has a "boyfriend closet." There she keeps boxes, all arranged and alphabetized, containing mementos of past loves. Photographs, theater ticket stubs, Hallmark cards, each collection organized by boyfriend, like old school books you might want to one day refer to. "Wow," I'll say, seeing this. I don't have a boyfriend closet. I don't arrange my lessons that way. Mine blend more spontaneously into my basement and my attic and my heart.

Anyway, I now own a groundhog video. I keep it by the TV. Sometimes people ask me why I have a groundhog video there. I tell them I don't really have any other place to put it.

Bargemen of the Monongahela 8

The cook aboard the *Spike Crain* already had lost four pairs of bifocals to the river. She was 54 years old, had a wiry head of blonde hair, and a nose too steep to hold up the glasses. Visitors were not usually invited to board the *Spike Crain* without someone in management asking the cook to please watch her language.

"But I said, 'bullshit with that,'" the cook told me. She was standing in the galley, washing dishes after a spaghetti and meatball dinner. "I can't be pretending to be something I'm not." For 12 years she had been working among a boatful of rivermen and, like them, she lived on the boat for 14 days at a time, and then had a week off to recuperate. "Swearing's a way of relieving tension," she said, adding that it was an activity that even her priest had endorsed. "'They're man-made words,' he told me, 'ain't no God gonna send you to hell for man-made words.' Then he told me that if I was too worried about using them, I could say ten Hail Mary's after each one. But I said, 'bullshit with that,'" she said, and let loose a high-pitched giggle. It was about the only sound, since my arrival, that was able to pierce the roar of two diesel engines propelling the *Spike Crain* on and on and on like a bus stuck in low gear.

We had left Pittsburgh two days previously with seven empty barges, and presently were on our way up the Monongahela River to Morgantown, West Virginia. (You travel "up" the Mon when you are going south, since the Mon flows north. It is one of the few rivers besides the Nile to defy laws of gravity in such a disorienting way.) We were to drop off the empties in Morgantown, pick up seven loads of limestone, and bring them back to Neville Island.

The cook's name was Eve. She had changed her name from "Ethel" because "Ethel" reminded her of a cow. Someone had recently told her, though, that "Ethel" meant "noble," and so she was thinking of reclaiming the name. "That's what I am," she said, "a noble old cow."

Her galley was a well-stocked, clean and accommodating kitchen, and it had all the conveniences of a 1950s mobile home. No dishwasher, but a nice big double sink, a large refrigerator freezer, and a handsome range. The table sat four, and was covered by a flowered cloth. The spaghetti Eve served that evening was her mother's recipe, and so was the tuna casserole she had to make for Johnny Ray since he didn't like spaghetti. She also made sure to keep the cucumbers out of the salad since Tom couldn't stomach cucumbers. Eve aimed to please—but only, she was quick to point out, when it came to cooking and other domestic chores.

"The first thing I said when I came out here," she told me, "was 'I'll do my own blankin' work and you do yours. I'm not out here to entertain men.' I put my foot down in the very beginning and never had no trouble after that.

"They're good boys," she added. "This is good clean living out here."

A deckhand named John came into the galley to help himself to a glass of Kool-Aid and he told Eve that the spaghetti that night sure was delicious. She smiled at him. On his way out he emptied his glass of ice right down the back of her shirt. Four-letter word after four-letter word came in combinations you never thought possible, and John appreciated the show.

Four ornery deckhands, one outspoken cook, and two unlikely pilots drifted on toward Morgantown, passing by the mills and backyards of western Pennsylvania. They are the unnoticed neighbors.

Rarely do you see the full crew of a towboat in one place at the same time, since it usually is broken in two: a "forward-watch," and an "after-watch." One shift works while the other sleeps. The idea is to keep the boat moving 24 hours a day, seven days a week. During my visit on a hot and steamy week in July, the forward-watch on the *Spike Crain* was manned by Tom, Bernie and John.

"There is no place I'd rather be," Tom said, in one of the truest moments of sarcasm aboard the *Spike Crain*, "than right here tonight." It was nearly midnight, we had been held up in Morgantown for over an hour, and the sky had just let loose a crack of lightning.

"It's just heat lightning," John said, "it's not gonna storm."

"Yeah, we'll take your word for it," Tom said. "You and the weatherman."

Just then the rain came down.

"Must be heat drops," Tom said, and he ducked back in the pilothouse. He was the pilot and so he would stay dry. John was a deckhand, on duty, and the seven barges we were hitching to the towboat still weren't ready to go. John got drenched, and so did Bernie.

To understand what it's like to hitch seven barges to a towboat, you first have to realize that a towboat doesn't tow anything. It pushes, like a train would if all the power were put in the caboose. When a pilot steers a seven-barge hitch, he is looking out over two, four, six barges, and he has the odd one tied to his "wing," which is on the side of the boat. He is steering 525 feet of floating steel in front of him that must move as a unit; if it sways or splits or otherwise misbehaves, he could lose control of the boat. Barges need to be secured together tightly and a good deckhand knows how to do that, how to tie the right lines around the right timberheads and tighten the right cables with just the right ratchets and winches and cheeterbars. But a bad deckhand sometimes makes mistakes, which is apparently what had happened down in Morgantown. Seven barges of limestone had been left for our pickup, but whoever left them had failed to assemble them properly. And so for over an hour John and Bernie had been laboriously unhitching and rehitching them, so that the *Spike Crain* could be on its way back down the Mon.

They were meticulous about the job, despite the rain, the lightning, and the fact that, once finished, they would have to do it all over again in about an hour. After leaving Morgantown, the *Spike Crain* would approach Lock 8; its chambers were too small for our tow, indeed for any tow over two barges long. You have to double-lock at Lock 8, which is an incredibly frustrating ordeal. You have to separate your hitch, send half your barges through the lock, tie them up on the other side, bring the other barges through, and then put the whole juggled mess back together again. Two good deckhands can double-lock a seven barge hitch in about 45 minutes. Ten miles past Lock 8 comes Lock 7, with yet another undersized chamber, where the same painstaking annoyances repeat themselves.

If a deckhand gets grouchy or ornery or sometimes looks depressed, the reason may have something to do with the fact that he spends most of his day like a child trying to put together a jigsaw puzzle that somebody keeps coming by and messing up.

During a six-hour shift, your average deckhand smokes a full pack of cigarettes. He cannot drink any alcohol, even when he's off duty, because none is permitted on the boat, and because the boat rarely stops moving long enough for him to sneak ashore for even a quick nip. (The shores of the Mon offer few such temptations anyhow.) For Frank, a deckhand on the after-watch, a tall glass of Coke or Sprite or any old gingerale would have been a welcomed luxury. "I gotta have bubbles," he would say to me repeatedly. "A guy down at Lock 4 is gonna have some pop for me when we get there. What kind of pop do you like? I can get you some. Any kind. Don't you need bubbles?"

Bernie, the forward-watch deckhand, was the new kid on the block, having worked the Mon less than six months. When he put on his life jacket, as all deckhands must do before they walk out on the barges, Bernie's didn't hang on him so much as it sat. He was a round man, big and sloppy like a bear, had blond hair, and he wore thick black glasses—the kind people attach noses to and wear as a joke. Always intent on getting the job done right, Bernie was one of the few deckhands you might see actually practicing on his time off. When an ordinary deckhand's shift is over, when he's through hooking timberheads, cranking winches, tightening cables, and getting all manner of grease trapped beneath his hopelessly dirty fingernails, he likes to go into the line room, scoop out a fantastic wad of "Shur Kleen," and massage it through his hands. He tries to forget about the diesel fumes that have already altered his sense of smell; he tries to forget about the constant drone of the twin screw engines that have made his voice hoarse from screaming over them. Showering, eating, then maybe taking an old newspaper or issue of *Playboy* out on a barge, he tries to relax like a man at home after a crummy day of work. Then he tries to sleep, while the towboat bumps his bunk continuously into the wall beside him.

But Bernie wasn't one to relax. Bernie liked to hone his skills, to throw a line over a timberhead, then step back, and see if he could do it over again from even further away. Bernie liked to coil lines, clockwise, endlessly, or else sit on the floor of the line room and weave eyes into the ends of poly-lines.

"It's like folding the laundry," he said to me. "You take the time to figure out how to do it right, and then you don't ever have to iron." He was standing out on number 910, a standard 175 foot by 26 foot barge, and he had one line coiled over each shoulder, wearing them like a coat. They were fore-and-aft lines, and they weighed about 50 pounds each, maybe 75 when wet.

John, who was lanky, blond, and who seemed never to have escaped a happy adolescence, was out on 910, too, when I made the ridiculous mistake of stepping on one of 910's hatch covers. John gasped, Bernie snapped at me, and they told me never to step on a hatch cover again. I said I was sorry, and then wondered why I was apologizing.

Hatch covers can come loose, Bernie told me, and a person could tumble right down inside the dark corridor that lines a barge. It is the crawl space of a barge, the place a deckhand must go to check for leaks in a barge, where he takes his broom and shovel and pump and sloshes his way through gravel and mud and all manner of mysterious debris hidden by the darkness.

"Sometimes," Bernie said to me, "when I'm down in there, I start imagining things." He was cranking a ratchet and the rain made his hair stick flat to his head. "I imagine, in the darkness, a hand coming from nowhere and grabbing hold of my ankle."

John insisted that I go down and see what it was like for myself. Had it not been midnight and had a thunderstorm not just passed overhead, and had I trusted John a little bit more, and had Bernie at least offered to go with us, I may have been a little less hesitant, but in any case I went down inside 910.

John and I descended a rusty ladder into a hallway that could just as easily have been a dungeon. The air was thick, moist and sickening, and since it was so dark in there and I couldn't see anything anyhow, I said maybe I didn't need to look around anymore.

"I always think of it as a great hideaway," John said, adding that he thought about it every time he passed the state penitentiary near Neville Island. "It's the perfect escape for a prisoner," he said, and his voice was echoing. "A guy can just swim out to the barge, open the hatch cover, and hop in. Hell, he could live down in here—if the rats didn't bother him too much."

I said I understood where Bernie got the paranoia about the hand grabbing his ankle, and we climbed back up the ladder.

We were three kids at summer camp telling horror tales on a lonely Friday night. John was the instigator, Bernie the serious boy, and I was trying my hardest not to be squeamish. I was wet and cold and dirty all the way through my clothes, which is okay, if that's how you like to play. But John and Bernie were the same way, night after day after night, covered by grease and rust and sweat and not even able to go home and forget about it all, not even able to make a phone call to a friend, a wife, a lover, just to say, "I feel awful," and to receive a single word of comfort. I wondered how they could be so complacent, living with the droning engines more often than they lived without them.

Later that night, it must have been 3 A.M., John and I stopped in the galley for some Kool-Aid, taking a quick break after Lock 8. John was telling me about his brother who worked as an accountant. "He's gotten so damn used to that air conditioning," he said. "Guys like him get home and they can't even go outside because it's too hot out. But they play golf. They play racquetball and they lift weights. I don't know, it's weird, the way they live," he said.

"Out here, there's no traffic and you don't have to deal with a lot of people, just six at a time. You sit and watch the water. You think. You think a lot. Then you go home and you can be in the mountains for a whole week. You get away there, too.

"It's a way of getting away."

In his autobiography, Mark Twain said that when he was first learning how to steer a steamboat, he realized he was ill-equipped for the job. "I haven't got brains enough to be a pilot," he confessed to one old captain, "and if I had I wouldn't have strength enough to carry them around, unless I went on crutches."

Captain Fred Way, a retired packet boat pilot, is known as the Mark Twain of the Monongahela, Allegheny and Ohio Rivers, and he wrote about the mystique of the river pilot in a similar way, saying that it takes a special breed of man to do the job. "You can't *make* a pilot out of *anybody*; a man has to have it born in him; pilotin' comes natural." (At 84, Fred Way has just published his eighth book. "It weighs four and a half pounds," he attests, "don't drop that on your foot.")

Less lyrical, but equally telling, is the opinion offered by a more modern-day pilot, Captain Ernie Higgs, a 65-year-old riverman who steers the boats of Pittsburgh's Gateway Clipper Fleet. "Working the rivers is kind of a real man's job," he said one night when he was docking the *Gateway Party Liner*. The barge he was towing was filled to capacity with a group of young singles, plus at least four elderly women on the middle deck playing gin. "You love the river," he said. "And steering the boat is a way of being in charge of it all. I used to get a kick out of the little kids who came on board and said, 'hey mom, there's the captain!' And I tell my deckhands that story. I say, 'some day, instead of being down there, you can be up here and be the captain.'" Larry Lee Jones and his country western band were the featured entertainers that evening. Docking the boat, Captain Higgs was looking out over the singles who, at some point in the evening, had become couples, and had moved to the upper deck for a more passionate end to the evening. But Captain Higgs paid them no mind. He called orders down to his deckhands, and, with the tunes of Larry Lee Jones thumping through the pilothouse, he tapped his foot to the beat. "And the little kids will say, 'hey mom, hey pop, there's the captain!' It could be you."

They each steered very different kinds of boats, but, ultimately, Mark Twain, Fred Way and Ernie Higgs chose the same word to describe the river pilot. "He was king," they each said. And every deckhand wanted to be a pilot as much as princes dream of one day acquiring the throne.

The crew of the *Spike Crain* did not quite fit into that classic pattern, however.

When Johnny Ray was steering the boat, Bernie assumed a gait that came to be known as "the crab walk." Bernie would cramp his knees low to the floor and waddle about like a duck, ready to hit the deck at any instant. Johnny Ray had a way of bumping, of steering full-throttle right into the wall of a lock, just to make sure he was on target. It was enough to knock a deckhand right into an empty barge, especially a new deckhand like Bernie, who hadn't yet developed his river legs. Once, when Eve was frying chicken down in the galley, Johnny Ray bumped so hard that the whole pot of grease came flying out of the pan, just missing Eve's face. "He knew I was frying chicken down here—I know he did. I went up to that pilothouse and I said, 'what's the matter Johnny, don't you like me?'"

Bumping, as it turns out, is not so much a sign of a pilot's skill as it is a good indication of how well a pilot respects his crew.

At 62, Johnny Ray had a reputation for being a crotchety old captain who never had a whole lot to say to anyone, except when he was firing orders down to his crew. He was a round-shouldered man and his body, having filled out over the years, was contained by the great swivel chair in the pilothouse like a loaf of bread in a loaf pan. His face was covered by dry, almost cracking wrinkles, and when he managed a smile it was with great difficulty; Johnny Ray had little patience for fun and games. Other pilots, for instance, sometimes liked to dress up the pilothouse, but Johnny Ray would have none of it. Tom once put bicycle streamers—the kind kids attach to handlebars—on the ends of the boat's steering levers, but Johnny Ray ripped them off. Tom once brought in a plastic steering wheel from off a baby's carseat, hooked it to the control panel, and Johnny Ray took that away, too. Tom once painted the whole console in the pilothouse pink, and Johnny Ray ordered his deckhands to grab their brushes and bring up a bucket of fresh white paint.

Johnny Ray started working the rivers in 1947, when steamboats were the common vessel, and men were men. "It was a different kind of work," he told me one night. "Oh yeah, these deckhands we got today woulda never made it on the steamboats. We used to have iron men and wooden hulls, and now we got iron hulls and wooden men," he said, and told me it was a saying a lot of old rivermen used. He was working his way through a pack of generic menthol cigarettes. During a six-hour shift, your average pilot smokes about the same amount as your average deckhand, the only difference being that a pilot smokes every cigarette down to the butt. Deckhands usually pitch theirs into the river after a few draws, when their hands become too occupied with matters of hooking and cranking and coiling.

"Very few of these deckhands out here become pilots anymore," Johnny Ray continued. "They don't take an interest in it. They don't want the responsibility, I guess. It's the kids today, you know, I mean, they don't got no ambition. It's every place," he said. He was sitting in the darkened pilothouse, leaning back, one finger on the steering lever, a short-wave radio mumbling Coast Guard weather reports, the diesel engines droning, and the river before him as idyllic as an interstate highway.

Johnny Ray had a farm in Punxatawny that interested him far more than did the mighty Mon.

When I asked John and Bernie and the *Spike Crain*'s other two deckhands, Mike and Frank, if they hoped to become pilots, they all said no. They were not putting in time on barges just so they could one day move upstairs, out of the rain, into a comfortable pilothouse. They did not consider themselves apprentice pilots. They did not consider themselves confirmed and committed deckhands, either. Nor were they particularly passionate about the Allegheny, the Ohio, the Monongahela or any other river.

Bernie was an ex-Navy man who, he said, had warned the Navy that he was getting a little sick and tired of all the orders from above, of the constant commands, of the utter lack of freedom, and when the Navy didn't listen, he up and quit. John was an ex-steelworker who, one day in the mills, discovered his own epilepsy; the attack frightened him and everyone around him and made unemployment a near certainty for him. Frank was a straight "A" student who had chosen not to go to college; he didn't like his father's idea of a career path and one day he told his father the same thing Bernie told the Navy. Mike was an ex-Coast Guard engineer who finally became obsessed with the notion that he was not allowed to get a sunburn on his own back, because his own back was considered government property.

To hear the deckhands of the *Spike Crain* talk about it, the river has no mysterious lure. The water doesn't pull you in; the land pushes you out.

The cook would probably agree. Eve had worked most of her life as a nurse; she had seven children from a long list of marriages and love affairs. One of her sons was a mulatto, and Eve's mother refused to even acknowledge him, as did a few of her friends and ex-husbands and past lovers. The one man she ever truly loved wouldn't love her back, and he broke her heart over and over again, until she was pretty well shattered. Then came the final blow: an automobile accident that forced Eve to stay in a hospital, flat on her back for nine months. "And I laid in that hospital, and I figured out my life," she told me. "I decided that I don't need no men. I don't need to be beaten up and I don't need to be hurt. I'll just forget them all."

"Out here I forget everybody and everything. Out here, this is my family."

The river took on a wholly different character when Tom was steering the boat. It became an interesting river, full of signs and history and adventure, and the pilothouse became a living room. With Tom in the pilothouse the crew would sit together and watch the shores go by, in silence, until suddenly Tom would pick out a point in the landscape and talk a blue streak about it. Tom could tell you the whole history of a log cabin built by a 70-year-old man; he could tell you the mechanical intricacies of the trams that run through West Virginia University; he could tell you about the problems of the folks living in a passing trailer park. The accuracy of the stories never seemed to matter much to anyone. We passed a duck swimming along with her four ducklings and Tom lifted his binoculars, watched them, and then told us all about ducks. We sat behind him, facing his back, all of us looking at the river, like friends watching home movies.

Tom had curly locks of grey hair, and a figure like a golfer's. He wore red suspenders and when he turned around you saw a bulbous nose and a t-shirt that read, "if you can't dazzle 'em with brilliance, baffle 'em with bullshit." He began telling us a story about Bill, a deckhand everyone knew, who once got confused in an airport in Canada.

"So here's Bill, okay? He's late for this plane and he's runnin' through this Canadian airport. He jumps on this escalator goin' down, right? Wrong. The escalator was headin' up. But old Bill, he was still headin' down.

"So here's Bill, tumblin' down this up-escalator, okay? Well, with them steps comin' up at him, he couldn't get to the bottom. He could've tumbled on forever and ever."

Eve was in the pilothouse and her giggle was in rare form, and Mike and Frank were enjoying the show too. We were headed for Maxwell Lock and Dam, having already passed through Lock 4, where Frank had stocked the refrigerator with enough bubbles to last us all a week. Presently, we were relaxing after a hearty meal of stuffed peppers, homemade bread, homemade bread pudding, and plenty of other carbohydrates. Eve was a little disappointed that no one ate the celery stuffed with peanut butter, but at the moment she was terribly concerned about Mike. She had given him a haircut earlier that day in the galley, and didn't like what she saw.

"It's thinning," she told me. "I think that damn Head & Shoulders is what did it. You know, his father's not bald.

"Mike, are you still using that Head & Shoulders?" she asked, and leaned over to check his scalp.

"C'mon Eve," Mike said, and he pushed her hand away. He was a handsome man of about 30, his hair was dark, and he looked more like a businessman than a deckhand. Mike wore a constant sneer on his face that made him seem always to be thinking, "this just isn't fair."

"I thought I told you to stop using that shampoo!" Eve said. "You know, your father's not bald. You shouldn't go bald, Mike. But I could see a lot of hairs missing, Mike. Have you been using conditioner? You know, if you would just use a little conditioner, just twice a week, it would help. And if you would just throw out that damn Head & Shoulders."

"C'mon, Eve, lay off, will ya?" Mike said.

"Look at Frank's hair," she continued. Frank had thick golden locks that hung below his shoulders. "Look at all that *hair*! It's pretty Frank, it's really pretty. Wouldn't you like to have hair like that, Mike?"

"You better lay off Eve," Tom put in, warning her. "You don't know what these guys will do if you get them angry."

"Oh, I know," she said, looking around, and she mumbled a little. "I know what they do. Do you wanna hear what they do, Tom? They rip the last page of my novel right out of the book, that's what they do! Those punks. Did you hear about that Tom? I read the whole damn book and never did find out how it wound up. Those punks.

"But I always did say," she said, sighing, then pushing her glasses up her nose, "I always did say, 'I'm the Happy Cooker around here. Just the Happy Cooker.'

"Oh, I love that house right there," she said, pointing her finger off to shore. "Isn't that right, Tom? Boy, they really fixed that up nice, didn't they Tom?"

Tom's turn to take the floor was long overdue, and the best way to take the floor from Eve was to tell stories about her. Tom told us drinking stories, about taking Eve out bar-hopping with the guys, as he often did when he was home. He said that Eve had a drinking problem and he said it had nothing to do with alcoholism. He said Eve had a way of falling asleep when she drank, and he said she always managed to fall asleep in a certain ladies room in a truck stop near Monessen. "So I have to climb over, hold on, and look down, and there's old Eve, passed out again on the hopper. I wake her up, I walk out of this damn ladies room, and I'll tell you them truckers give me some pretty heavy looks."

Except for her giggle, the story shut Eve up.

Outside, John and Bernie were three barge-lengths away; they were perched on two timberheads, where all would be still and quiet. Out there, you can't hear the drone of the engines or Eve's giggle, and you can't even smell the diesel. Sometimes you smell honeysuckle and sometimes you hear someone laughing on shore or a child crying. The barges push through the water and you watch the water; you wonder how deep it is, how cold it is, or just how it would feel to suddenly dive in. Once, when I was out there with them, John and I heard something rustling in the bushes; we looked left, and we saw a six-point buck hobbling through the brush that met the shore. The deer had been shot—we could see the wound—by someone who apparently thought that hunting season was a year-round thing. For a good hour we talked about how unfair that was, and we said we hoped the hunter never found the deer when it finally died, that he never got the chance to show the six points off to his neighbors, and we said that we hoped the deer would die soon. We also found a box turtle caught between two barges, where rubble often collects.

Maxwell Lock was a beauty. A clean, white, tidy, double-chambered 84-by-720-foot-concrete sight for sore eyes. It put our rusty 910 and 812 barges to shame, but nonetheless allowed us to sail right through in one trip like a dream. Going through, Tom and the rest of us sat in the pilothouse and laughed at the lockmen. They have a certain look, lockmen; a way of suggesting models in brochures for industrial safety equipment. They spend their entire working day catching lines from deckhands, hooking them to timberheads, then walking 525 feet, catching more lines from more deckhands, and hooking them to more timberheads. To help them out with this, the U.S. Army Corps of Engineers has provided them with golf carts, thus minimizing the stress from the walk between timberheads.

"Don't strain yourselves, guys!" Tom called out.

"Hell, how do you think I got this?" one called to us, and he pointed to a belly that sat on his lap like a watermelon. "Thirteen years I been out here," he said, and he threw a *Pittsburgh Press* down to Bernie, who was on the lower deck, wearing the life preserver that sat on him, and the black glasses that reminded you of dumb jokes.

"What a rut," Tom said about the lockmen's idea of a day of work. "A lotta guys ask me how I can stand my job," he said, and that inspired him to offer his "rut" theory. "What I tell my friends when they ask me how I can live out here, I say, 'I bet I can tell you where you'll be on a Friday night at 8. You'll be in a bar, right?' And they say yes, and that's when I tell them they're in a rut, see? Why do you have to drink at 8 on a Friday night? You don't. You can drink at 8 on a Monday morning if you want to, if you're not in a rut. Out here, you don't get in a rut," he said.

He never did conclude the story about Bill, who could very well still be tumbling down an up-escalator, somewhere in an airport in Canada, stuck in a rut of the most absurd variety.

"I could jump off this boat and be home in 45 minutes," Tom said. He had settled into his chair, a cigarette hung from his mouth, his feet were resting on the instrument panel, and he was looking off toward Canonsburg.

"I could jump off this boat and be home in 35 minutes," someone else said, and that was pretty much the way the conversation continued, as we plodded on down the Mon with our seven loads of limestone.

"It's pretty bad when you buy a brand new four-wheel-drive and you don't even get to use it. It's a Dodge Aspen. It's sitting there on the street at home."

"I could keep a girlfriend if I was home."

"I could jump off this boat and be home in 20 minutes."

"I have enough bubbles to last me 'till next Tuesday, when I'll go home and get bubbled out."

"The married guys want to get off at a lock and call home— especially on a Friday or a Saturday night. They make the call and they don't get no answer. They come back on the boat, swearin' and kickin' the deck."

"I could jump off this boat and be home in 10 minutes."

"You couldn't blame her. I was never home. I was always out here on this boat."

In an issue of *The Waterways Journal*, there is a front page advertisement for a company that repairs towboats. "We fix everything about a vessel," it reads, "except a cook's broken heart."

It would be difficult to find another business that, in 1984, could get away with a statement like that. But towing barges is a way of life that has, ever since the diesel engine took over for steam, effectively escaped modernization. You do things by hand on the *Spike Crain*. Your tools, the ratchets and winches and cheeterbars, are about as high-tech as the medieval ball-and-chain, and just about as cumbersome. The sudden rage on towboats around Pittsburgh is the electric winch, and it is changing the way a deckhand thinks about tightening a cable. Just a push of a button and that winch cranks all by itself, like magic. The *Spike Crain* has already been fitted for a set of electric winches; any day they could arrive.

Soon also—and this is highly controversial—the *Spike Crain* may get microwave ovens. Eve told me about them one day, at around 5 A.M., when she was in the galley frying up some bacon. Eve was an amazingly talkative person at 5 A.M. She was telling me first about her nose, saying the reason it was so slanted was because it was badly broken in the car accident. "My whole face got rearranged," she said, "I didn't used to look like this, you know." She also told me that the accident left her with a scar that ran down the whole front of her body. Laying in the hospital for nine months, she thought about that scar, about turning it into a snake and then making a career as an exotic dancer. But that idea never panned out, she said, and instead she came out to the river, and, in any case, the doctor did a miserable job on her nose and so for the rest of her life she would be losing bifocals to the river.

That was when she began telling me about the microwaves. "They want to get rid of the cooks out here," she said. "We're too expensive," she said. "They can save a hell of a lot of money by just putting in microwaves and letting these guys cook for themselves."

"It would be a real tragedy," she said. "Terrible. All the guys say so. Cause you know what will happen. You'll get riff-raff. You'll get a bunch of I-don't-cares out here. You won't get the same quality person out here." She was pointing her knife at me, bouncing it, lecturing me. Behind her was a wooden cannister set that Tom had made. He had burned the words "Spike Crain" into the wood, the same way they do to those personalized plaques you can get at the mall. The smell of bacon was a good contest for the diesel fumes, and, since the boat was not yet near Pittsburgh, the shores were dark and still.

"We used to have some riff-raff out here," she said. "The older men, you know. I remember one pilot sitting in that pilothouse with his privates exposed, just so I would see. I complained about it, but the management said, with my mouth, what should I expect?

"That was when I first started out here, and I've seen those guys leave. But you get rid of me, and they'll come back.

"I go, and this whole damn river goes to the riff-raff."

The Pig Man 9

As a pig racer, somewhat famous and content, Merle Mills looks at the human journey this way: "Who the hell knows what you're gonna do in life?"

Recently I got to know Merle, having spent the night with him, plus ten of his pigs. Merle slept up in the truck; I was back in the trailer, eyes wide open and confused: "What am I doing here?" The pigs were in the trailer with me, beyond a wall, piled one on top of the other in a big lump. Pigs, apparently, sleep this way. We were parked in an otherwise deserted shopping center, and it was raining outside. The trailer was jet black and enormous—42 feet long—and to a passerby it might have looked handsome and lonely, like an art deco diner.

Towing this trailer full of pigs, Merle and I were traveling on a journey together, two shy strangers headed south.

I had heard about Merle, the quiet man people had come to call The Pig Man. He lived in Germantown, Maryland, and most of his life he had worked as a plumber. But about five years ago, he discovered the secret to training pigs, and ever since he's been going from state fair to county fair to state fair, up and down the east coast, with his pigs. "Dash for Mash" is what Merle calls his act. He's booked solid through this summer and into next. Last year he began racing ducks and pygmy goats. Sometimes he thinks: What if you could get a chicken to roller skate?

Merle Mills is 57, mostly bald, rather short and packed solidly. His skin is deeply tanned, and blue eyes jump out of his plain face with a holler. He wears a khaki shirt and trousers, carries an extra set in a brown paper bag. Merle moves through life at such an odd pace, I thought. Here was a man with a gypsy spirit. I had never been on a journey with a gypsy before.

"Oh, hell, you sleep in the trailer; I'll sleep in the truck," Merle had said to me, apologizing for the fact that we had no light, no heat, no water, no food—except for a box of Doo Dads, the Nabisco party snack.

"Lock the door!" he had shouted, putting me in the trailer.

Neither of us said good night, since it seemed too personal and, anyhow, too impossible.

The pigs had a good night, I think; it's hard to tell. While nestled in their one great blubbery lump, one of the pigs on the bottom would occasionally need to move, disturbing the whole pile of pigs, which would all have to pile themselves up again, rocking the trailer back and forth like a boat. I tried to sleep, lying beneath a damp blanket, shivering, wearing all of my clothes, including my sneakers in case something happened and I had to run.

Would we make it to Smithfield? This had been the main question ever since we left Merle's farm, at 4 P.M. on a Saturday. We were bound for Smithfield, North Carolina; the Smithfield

Ham and Yam Festival was an annual event that this year would feature Merle's racing pigs. The gig would mean $1,000 to Merle; it would have meant $1,500 if his wife hadn't handled the booking. Merle usually charges more if he has to drive far.

Things began gloomy, got gloomier. The rain out of Washington had been heavy. The truck was acting up, bucking, and I could see plainly, early on, that the clutch was giving Merle a good fight.

He didn't worry about it; he didn't seem to worry about much. Merle moves so casually from one moment to the next that in his world any emergency is fixable with a wrench and a rag; you deal with it when it happens. So he kept fighting his clutch in a private kind of way, not complaining, while we talked about pig racing.

"It's here to stay," he said, hollering over the roar of the engine. "Like the merry-go-round and the Ferris wheel, pig racing is here to stay." He said he didn't invent pig racing, but he is only the second one to do it. Having raised hogs all his life, Merle decided to train them at the urging of the manager of the Montgomery County Agricultural Fair. Hazel Staley had seen "Heinold Downs," a pig-racing show in the Midwest, and she wanted to try a similar thing back home. She went to Merle, a friend who frequently showed hogs at the fair. "She talked me into trying to race them," Merle told me. "And she's the type that don't take no for an answer; she cracks down on you, and you almost gotta do it to get her off your back. So I told her I'd try it, but we wouldn't say nothing to nobody because if it didn't work, you know, I didn't want people to think I was a damn fool."

It worked. At the 1984 Montgomery County Fair, Merle's pigs were received with resounding enthusiasm, which five years later is still resounding. Merle himself has some trouble understanding this. "I don't know," he said. "Everyone loves a pig, I guess."

He looked at me, smiled, shrugged, then coughed, pulled out a cigarette, a filterless Camel. He told me about a fair he went to in New Jersey a couple of years back: "The governor flew in, and his stage was right next to mine. And he was a little late. So they stopped my pig race when he arrived. And I tell you, if I was governor, I woulda got back in that damn helicopter and flew off. They booed that man. They actually booed him because he stopped the pig race. The people was some kinda upset.

"Everyone loves a pig."

Merle's truck finally gave up, at Lane 12 in a tollbooth near Richmond. Merle went at it with his wrench. "The whole damn thing is made of plastic," Merle said to the tollbooth man, who had a scab on his nose and a hefty cigar in his mouth and who welcomed our breakdown with joy. "Ha, ha, ha! You're stuck! Er, I mean, it's not funny, but . . ."

The clutch was stuck, to the floor. It was a hydraulic clutch, made of one piece of plastic. You couldn't take it apart. Here was a problem Merle couldn't fix. Here was a man meeting his limitations. He had an odd grin on his face.

"At least you're not raising hell," the tollbooth man said.

"No sense in it," Merle said, sitting there, thinking. He pumped the clutch, hoping for magic. It worked. We made it to the next tollbooth, where we broke down again, met a new toll taker, plus a man in a brown van who offered help. The man could not talk, only grunt, a problem that proved frustrating for all of us because the man seemed to have some definite knowledge of hydraulic clutches. He grunted. Merle said, "Huh?" This happened many times, until we were on our way again.

Stopping and starting and getting help from strangers, this is how we proceeded on our journey. The strangers, it seemed, all had problems, like that man who could only grunt. A Vietnam vet who helped under the hood said his right leg was not a real leg. A hotel maid who gave us a lift went on and on about how she had run out of linens. We met a lot of people like this.

Somewhere along the way, I figured out we weren't going to get dinner, so I ran in and bought the Doo Dads.

Merle grew up on a farm, about two miles down the road from where he lives now. "I never went far," he said. Like a lot of farm kids, he wanted nothing to do with farming when he became a man. He got a job. "I started out with a pick and shovel," he said. "Really, that was the easiest job I ever had."

He dug ditches. "Somebody told you where to dig, how much to dig and when to stop. And if you got it dug, you got it dug. If not, you caught hell." Life was a very simple equation back then. "But it wasn't satisfying," he said. "I wanted to be boss."

He went off to war, came back, and by the 1960s he had become boss. He oversaw 100 men at times, working on the plumbing of large buildings. "Hell, I'll never go back to fooling with 100 men," he told me. "It's not worth it."

About his new life as a pig racer, he said, "This is just me. What I do, I do."

All of his equipment was designed and built in his backyard. He made the racing track out of pipes and plumbing joints. He built the starting gate out of refrigerator shelves. He attached a bell to it. He took some six-inch plastic PVC pipe, cut it, covered it with canvas, sewed some felt numbers onto it and thus had himself some smart-looking racing saddles for his pigs to wear.

Merle told me he learned a few important lessons, training his pigs. In the beginning, he worked hard, encouraged them, tried to get them to run together in one direction. "But them little jokers would keep turning around," he explained. The pigs would come back, stand there, look at him. He wanted them to run! He wanted them to race! He wanted them to be trained athletes! He worked and worked with them. "Let's go! Let's go!" But the pigs would just stand there, look at him, like, "Give it up, Mister."

So he did. "Hell, I found out, just let them play. They're gonna do it, you know?" He let them do it their way instead of forcing them to do it his way. The pigs wanted to play. They wanted to sniff around and check the track out, lay claim to the turf. Having given them this freedom, Merle discovered: "Then all you gotta do is step on the track and clap your hands, and them little jokers will go woof, woof, woof around the track. Because they had their little play out there. See, they taught me that. After they taught me what I was supposed to do, we got along fine."

And so he surrendered to a higher boss: his pigs. And it worked. Merle became a pig racer. He bought the trailer, the truck, fixed it all up his way and set out on the road. He didn't look back, didn't return to plumbing; pig racing was too good to be true. "It's so universal," Merle said. "You can work it any way you want and nobody kicks up a stink."

The Smithfield Ham and Yam festival was to be held at the Carolina Pottery Outlet Center, just off I-95, the flyer said. We rolled into it, barely, at around midnight. But the shopping center was empty. There were no banners. No hams. No yams. Nor were there any hotels in sight. And here the clutch quit for good. We were stuck.

So this is how it happened; this is how I came to sleep in a pig trailer parked in an otherwise-deserted shopping center, with ten pigs and a box of Doo Dads. I felt dirty, cold, crummy. And yet I felt strangely invigorated. Free. Like a gypsy, I guess. You surrender to a higher boss—a pig, the wind, the stars, a clutch—and you feel free.

In the morning, Merle woke up. He pounded on the door. "Good morning. How did you sleep? Like hell, I bet."

"I kind of drifted in and out," I said. "How about you?"

"Drifted in and out," he said.

"You must have been cold," I said.

"I got up and walked around," he said.

Before long, the Smithfield Jaycees arrived and began setting up their booths: ring toss, go fish, balloon darts. We were here! The wind had blown us to the right place after all. The Ham and Yam Festival was blooming all around us.

The pigs Merle races are young, retiring at the age of just three months. Back home, his wife trains the new ones, and Merle sweeps by and picks these up. He goes through five sets of pigs a season. "I like a young pig," he told me.

Retired racing pigs get sent to a feedlot and end up as sausage, tripe, fertilizer.

Merle's wife is named Frances, and she is a neat and tidy woman who keeps a spotless house. No pigs are allowed inside, Merle told me, adding that Frances nearly threw a fit the time he brought the pony in. Frances and Merle were high school sweethearts, got married young, had one son, and both agree that the only bad part of Merle's new career is that they get separated for weeks, sometimes months at a time, during fair season, when Merle is on the road. Frances looks at Merle in an adoring kind of way. Merle says, "Yeah, yeah, we get along good."

Two things Merle found interesting about the Smithfield Ham and Yam Festival: Number one, there never were any hams. Number two, there never were any yams. Apparently, all the food action happened the day before. Pig racing was the big event that Sunday, and there even was a comedian from "Hee Haw" there to emcee the event. There were also t-shirts with hams and yams pictured on them, and, of course, the Jaycee gaming booths, and down by the Cloud Nine yogurt store, the Smithfield-Selma Middle School Knights Band played "I Heard It Through the Grapevine."

The pig races happened every half hour, and indeed the pigs were crowd pleasers. Merle would sound his prerecorded bugle call, and all through the parking lot it would be heard. People would run, shouting, "The pig races!" dropping the Jaycees' balloon darts and leaving the school band right in the middle of a refrain.

It takes the pigs about 11 seconds to get around the track; then the race is over. Five pigs run around a 150-foot oval, at the end of which is food; basically what happens in a pig race is you let the pigs out to eat—just like the human race, only shorter. You go in a circle, and then you eat. You keep yourself alive. It's a routine.

The trimmings are what make the show so compelling: the bugle call, the bell, the starting gate, the adorable saddles, the crowd, the cheering, the emcee. And the fact that pigs look very funny running together.

"And they're off! Pig number two, pig number three by a nose, pig number one coming around the far turn, pig number three and pig number two nose to nose, oink to oink, pig number five, number one, number four, number two in last place and pig number three! Pig number three is our winner! Pig number three is represented today by Toy Liquidators. . . ."

It went on like this every 30 minutes, each pig representing a different store at the shopping center, and all the people cheering, slapping their knees. "This is so funny!" they would shout, watching the journey happen.

Sometime during the day—in between the races, and under the hot sun beating down on the asphalt, and among all the cheerful people playing games, winning prizes, winning goldfish in plastic bags—Merle fixed his clutch. The Vietnam vet, who knocked on his leg for us all to hear, helped Merle out with this. Together they plugged a plastic line, which turned out to have holes in it, leaking a trail of fluid all the way from Washington to Smithfield, apparently.

On the way back, we made it pretty far. And this time Merle even thought to stop for dinner. We went into the 76 Auto Truck Stop, passing some lawn sculpture: a giant Yogi Bear and a giant Boo Boo. Yogi had a chicken leg. Inside, Merle had chopped steak. I asked him how come he never worries.

"I used to worry," he said. "Like with the pigs. I used to worry they wouldn't do it right. But I found out whatever they do, people like them anyhow, so why worry about it?

"I used to worry," he went on. "And things used to make me so damn mad. Oh, I can get stinking mad. Like I used to yell at the men in construction. Yell at them for no reason, just yell. Like I say, I would never go back to construction. I feel better now."

For the first time during our journey, he seemed eager to talk: "It's a shame you can't do this when you're younger, just enjoy life, then settle down and work when you get old." He took a forkful of mashed potatoes.

"Today everybody just works, works, works. Really, you know a lot of them work two or three jobs. It's really to get what they want—that's the reason they have to work. It's not to live. It's to get what you want. There is so damn much out there. Really, I think the want part is getting worse and worse. See, and maybe I'm old-fashioned. When we started out, there wasn't so much to want. There isn't much I want."

Doesn't he have a dream? Don't all gypsies have dreams?

He told me about the peanut man. It might, in truth, be better to be a peanut man than a pig man, he said. The peanut man had stopped by to see Merle earlier that day, and Merle was thinking about him. "He goes around, and he roasts peanuts. Big peanuts, you know. They're raw, 100-pound bags. Now he's got a really nice trailer, you know. You know that's a good way to get out and see the country. It's not a whole lotta work. You got a motor home, some peanuts, and you just work your way from fair to fair across the country. You know, you get to the other side, and you just work your way back. Roasting peanuts for the people. Put the side up, sell them, put the side down, go off and look the countryside over. It would be really great."

Hauling a 42-foot trailer, Merle has to stay on highways. He says all he's gotten to see of this country on his journeys these past four years is a white line in the middle of the night.

We got on our way, the white line that night still being I-95. We made it only to the second tollbooth. The clutch gave in again; this time, it seemed, the holes were too numerous to plug. It was midnight. Merle had a relative with a tow truck, called him. It would take the man about three hours to get to us. Merle leaned to the left, on his window. And so I leaned to the right, on my window.

"Well, good night," Merle said to me, and he folded his arms, shutting his eyes.

"Good night," I said.

A few silent moments passed, and then, in the darkness, out of nowhere, Merle began to laugh.

"It is funny, isn't it?" he said.

"It's really funny," I said, and I laughed, too.

I don't know what silly thing Merle found when he closed his eyes that night, but for me it was a distancing. I felt twice as dirty, twice as cold, twice as crummy as the night before, stuck in this truck with this stranger again, and these Doo Dads, and these pigs. "Who the hell knows what you're gonna do in life?" You surrender to a higher boss, surrender to the absurd, close your eyes to the whole mess, and laugh.

What's Lithuanian?   **10**

A young girl, perhaps seven years old, was peering down the west steps of the Capitol, wondering what all those people down there, chanting in protest, were yelling about. She couldn't understand their message, and so she asked her father: "Are they saying 'We-don't-know'?" It kind of sounded like that.

"No," her father said. "They're saying, 'Free-dom now!'"

The crowd below stood with flags, big flags, little flags, two flags, six flags, eight zillion flags it seemed. The overall effect was a sea of yellow, green and red stripes, all blowing to the right. The people began a new chant. "Nyet, nyet, Soviet!" Some held signs. "Same Crap, Different Czar," one read. "Don't Sell Democracy Support Lithuania," read another. "Oppression in Lithuania will not bring world peace," read a poster held by a priest who also wore a bumper sticker across his stomach: "No tanks in Lithuania." One old man, all alone, shuffled back and forth, a Soviet flag tied around his ankles.

The girl wanted to know who those people were.

"Lithuanians," her father said.

"What's Lithuanians?" she asked.

He seemed stumped. I thought it an appropriate response. I am stumped myself. Who are these people? I used to think I knew what a Lithuanian was.

It was a game to me. A funny thing. I loved saying it. With great pride I would announce to teachers and fellow classmates: "I am Lithuanian!"

"What's Lithuanian?" the other kids would ask.

"It's sort of like Irish or Italian," I would answer, "only it's Lithuanian." Being Lithuanian was a special thing, pure and simple. Because nobody else was Lithuanian. Because nobody ever even heard of it. Because it had to do with my family. "Is my dog Lithuanian?" I wondered back then, longing to understand just how the world was divided up.

And now look what's happened. The world is redividing itself, the Cold War having fizzled out, and we're all stumped, like curious children whose arms aren't long enough to get around an answer. Who are the good guys? Who are the bad guys? Where are we supposed to stand?

> *If you're true to yourself, how can you be indifferent? And now look what Bush is doing. Trade is more important to him. Trade? When it's the livelihood, the life itself, the lifeblood of a nation?*
>
> *I have screamed to my husband, I have cried, I have been frustrated, I have been tense, I have been depressed. And it's been in cycles. And one day I told my husband—I said, "I'm telling you in marital confidence: I'm ashamed to be an American."*
> —Danute Harmon, Falls Church, Virginia

When the Superpower summit blew through our nation's capital last month, clogging the streets like some really popular circus, people of Lithuanian descent came from all over North

America—nine busloads arrived from Chicago alone—to raise noise. They came to support the Lithuanian independence movement. To get some media attention. To show the people back in the homeland that even though our president isn't particularly vocal on this issue, some people in this great land of liberty support them. To shout to Gorbachev: "Liar! Hypocrite!" To shout to Bush: "Do something, you wimp!" To shout to the American public: "Stand up for your principles! Don't sell out!"

They were very excited. Did anyone even notice? They were a blip on the TV news, I think.

But the story was a lot bigger than a blip. I had come to see it for myself, because I am Lithuanian. And because I wanted to know what a Lithuanian is.

On the night of the first demonstration, the police kept order. "You Armenians are crazy!" a beefy cop yelled into the crowd. This was on 16th Street, about two blocks down from the Soviet Embassy. Gorbachev and Bush were due to drive by on their way to dinner. The people were gathered, hoping to be at least a flash in the corner of a president's eye.

"This is not Armenia!" a lady yelled to the beefy cop. "This is Lithuania! Don't you know your geography! Huh? Don't-you-know-your-geography?"

"I don't answer no questions," he said, and disappeared into a gathering of fellow cops. They rolled their eyes, sighed and discussed the situation among themselves. "These people are crazy," one said. "They're not so bad," responded another. "It's the anti-abortionists I hate. They come here like they got God on their side." Said another: "No, the gays are even worse." And another: "I don't mind the gays. The worst is the KKK. They bring so much hate."

You can tell a lot about a people's character, by its style of demonstrating; 16th Street that night was a dandy display of nationalism. Soon the Armenians arrived, and they filled in a small area inside the Lithuanians. Dark eyes, dark hair, they were fewer in number but much louder than the Lithuanians. Then came the Cubans, with darker complexions and fiery eyes and cries louder than even the Armenians'. This was all happening in front of the America's Best Contacts and Eyeglass store, where, as advertised, you could get "2 pair frames, plastic lenses, and eye exam $49.99 complete."

The Cubans decided to take on the cops, marching in unison; they were going to storm the Soviet Embassy!

No-they-most-certainly-were-not! The cops battled them back. There was a rumble. The Lithuanians, blond, fair-skinned, looked on. Their style was different. They swayed in unison. They held candles. They sang. One man looked up, as a helicopter flew overhead, and said simply: "Please, Mr. Bush, can you hear me? Free Lithuania."

"WHERE ARE THE LATVIANS?" a lost woman shrieked, her protest sign all bundled up in a blue bag. A car with a giant piece of broccoli on top came driving by, honking. "LaRouche says, Eat it George," the sign said. It was dusk.

Children found a grassy area and practiced cartwheels, one saying, "I did it!" and another answering, "No, you bent your legs."

The summit was in town and the whole world seemed topsy-turvy.

> *How can (the Lithuanians) back off? They think this would be a greater tragedy than the events of 1940 when they were invaded. Because, by suspending their declaration of independence and saying, "We will follow the Soviet constitution," they of their own free will would be saying "Yes, we are part of the Soviet Union." And they simply can't do that.*
> —*Victor A. Nakas, Falls Church, Virginia*

It used to be so much simpler. I knew what a Lithuanian was. I knew what the issues were. The main issue was: church clothes.

Did we have to wear them all day? We were going to Lithuania and I wanted to get changed.

Lithuania was where you went on Sundays, after church. We'd all pile into my dad's black Corvair convertible and leave our land of suburban happiness, where lawns were perfectly green and the sun shone perfect yellow, and we'd head on out, over the "stinky bridge" that spanned the oil refineries. There were no flowers where we were going, and no willow trees. Just people who spoke words I couldn't understand. It was a place of old people, tired people, worn-down people.

Like my grandparents. It was because of them, I was told, that I was Lithuanian. They spoke Lithuanian. They made Lithuanian foods, good bread and weird potato things, but mostly what we liked were the Milky Ways. My grandparents owned the corner grocery store and they'd give us meat and Milky Ways to take home, and my dad would stand by the car, shouting "No more Milky Ways! No more meat!" to my grandmother, who would keep coming out with boxfuls. And my grandfather would sit back and smoke, and my sister and I would twirl around the neighborhood, slapping our Sunday shoes on the pavement, and, breathless, we'd run up to all the neighbors. They were old people, sad people, sitting out on stoops. I wanted to cheer them up; I danced for them; I loved them. I loved this whole place—despite the oil refinery smell that made me sick, despite the itchiness I felt from wearing my church clothes, despite my frustration at never understanding a word anyone was saying. Lithuania was exotic compared with back home, where the lawns and the sun were. Lithuania was so romantic.

Some time later, my sister explained to me that this was not, in fact, Lithuania. This was South Philadelphia. My grandparents had fled Lithuania in the early 1900s, then settled in this tight Philadelphia neighborhood, an enclave of Lithuanian immigrants. The news came to me right about the time that Santa Claus was also found out.

Shattered fantasies leave an indelible mark on you, like a birthmark; you look at it and remember how you once were. Being Lithuanian is a birthmark on me.

Other people have it too, only I think they feel it many, many degrees more intensely than I do. For me, it has mostly been a romantic thing, a thing about childhood and innocence. It was a way for a young child to be special, distinctive, apart from the crowd. But when I came to Washington and went to the demonstrations, being Lithuanian became the opposite. It became a matter of figuring out how to join the crowd. Did I have the right? Compared with these people, I was a watered-down Lithuanian.

Many Americans of Lithuanian descent—there are at least 750,000 nationwide, with the biggest concentration in Chicago— tend to be rigid and passionate about holding on to their cultural heritage. These people grew up attending Lithuanian language classes on Saturdays, where they learned about their cousins back home, and where pride was instilled.

"We were brought up with the feeling that your aunts, your uncles, your cousins are living under occupation and it is your duty to maintain your cultural heritage," said Victor A. Nakas, Washington branch manager of the Lithuanian Information Center. "Because they are oppressed, and you are free, and you must not only speak out here in terms of the political situation, but you must also retain the language and know the culture. It was your duty."

"To us, this is the time we've been waiting for," said Darius Suziedelis, of the local chapter of the Lithuanian-American Community. There are 75 such chapters nationwide. "Our parents have been waiting for this time, our grandparents. This is our moment."

And so about 5,000 dutiful Lithuanians gathered in Washington that weekend.

They continued swaying and singing, there on 16th Street. Soon the Latvians and Estonians arrived, while the Cubans continued to take on the cops, and now the Armenians were cheering on the Cubans. "Go Cuba!" And the cops came at them with the dreaded yellow tape—"POLICE LINE DO NOT CROSS"— surrounding them. And the Lithuanians cheered on the Cubans. "Go Cuba!" There was confusion, until pretty soon everybody was back in place, and, as was surely inevitable that night, solidarity happened. Cubans, Armenians, Latvians, Estonians and Lithuanians joined forces, screaming together: "What do we want?"

"FREEDOM!"

"When do we want it?"

"NOW!"

The superpower motorcade made its way to the embassy, skipping that block, the presidents perhaps preferring not to deal with any of this nonsense.

> *Pure hypocrisy! And I'm FRUSTRATED. Because the American public is so easily duped by this charismatic character Gorbachev. They're duped. No wonder the kids are turned off and have taken to drugs. There's no leadership. No one standing for principles. Free Lithuania.*
>
> —*Antanas D'Alfonso, Philadelphia, Pennsylvania*

The word "Lithuania" keeps appearing on the front pages of newspapers, and every time I see it I feel an eerie, if undeserved, sense of pride. Like, that's my country. Like I'm playing a game of Risk, and this is my corner of the board. I am probably more of a Lithuanian fan than I am a Lithuanian.

The net effect is that I have taken a keen interest in the politics of Lithuania. Where should I stand? Where should any of us stand? It's not easy to figure out.

Some analysts thought the Lithuania question might become a pivotal one at the summit. (It didn't.) Could the United States sign a trade pact with a Soviet government that was suffocating a peaceful, freely elected democratic nation? In a confidential letter sent before the summit, Bush had warned Gorbachev not to expect him to sign, citing the public and congressional reaction to the economic blockade. (He signed.)

Not that this was a simple matter of national self-interest winning out over idealism. Well-intentioned leaders argue that, in the interests of disarmament and world peace, we'd better cheer Gorbachev on. They figure Gorbachev will eventually free the Baltic states, once the chaos in Eastern Europe settles down some. They figure the United States had better stay out of the Baltic independence movement, because any direct tampering might cause Gorbachev's demise—and who knows what kind of character might then come into power.

So we're walking on eggs, around the Lithuania issue. Here is a country which, first of all, was illegally annexed by the Soviet regime half a century ago. Between the two world wars, the Baltic countries were independent democracies. Then came the Hitler-Stalin pact, and they were occupied. Now Mikhail Gorbachev comes into power, saying this is the end of party rule; a constitutional government must prevail. So the Lithuanians abide by the constitution, and exercise their right to secede. On March 11, 1990, they claim their independence.

And Gorbachev says, "No. You must abide by the laws."

"What laws?" the Lithuanians wonder. Gorbachev writes some laws. "Approval by referendum is required," he says, in so many words, "plus a transitional period of up to five years, and then you'll need final approval by the Soviet Congress of People's Deputies, and, here you go, here are all the hoops you must dive through."

"Well, this is ridiculous," the Lithuanians respond. And they figure surely the Western world will agree. Surely the West will help out with this—not with arms, not with money, but with, simply, words. Words they had been using for half a century. Why should now be any different? For 50 years the United States has refused to recognize the annexation of the Baltic states. As far as the United States has been concerned, Lithuania, Latvia and Estonia were never part of the Soviet Union.

Now the Baltic countries are claiming their independence— announcing their very legitimacy—and what does the United States have to say? "Um, er, ugh." These are our new words. Gorbachev imposes economic sanctions, depriving Lithuania of fuel and food and medical supplies, and here we are just sort of ignoring all of that, like, well, we don't want to offend the man, and who are we to say what he does with his own country? And so we're shaking hands with him. Bringing him over for dinner. Giving him good deals on computers. Saying, yep, we're on your side. Nudge, nudge. But hey, you gotta work that Lithuania thing out, okay?

Who knows, maybe things will work out; as I write this, Gorbachev has at least agreed to negotiate with Baltic leaders. He even gave Lithuania a few tiny squirts of fuel, making, at least, a symbolic gesture of hope.

But I wonder how we Americans can really justify putting support for Gorbachev above the immediate freedom of the Baltic people. How can we take a neutral stance between freedom and tyranny?

> *America is all contrasts. In dress. In attitudes. In places you go. I was surprised to see this. I hope in ten years Lithuania can be like this. Not economically. We couldn't be. But morally. Spiritually. This is free. We don't have this.*
> *In Lithuania everything is all the same. Everything is down. Pushed down inside.*
> —Rita Sermuksnyte, Kaunas, Lithuania

I've been to Lithuania twice. The first time was in the mid-1980s when I toured the country along with my family. It's odd to take a trip with your family, as an adult. I'm not sure why my brother and sisters and I went, except we were curious, and I think we wanted to see my father look pleased. He had often talked about going to Lithuania.

The city of Vilnius, Lithuania's capital, was decorated. Big banners with the number 45 written on them adorned buildings, and enormous red 45 sculptures filled up whole city parks. This was the 45th anniversary of Lithuania's annexation, and, incredibly, the Soviets were celebrating it, sort of like throwing a big party on the anniversary of somebody's death.

Some of the banners featured giant, imposing pictures of Lenin, and giant imposing pictures of other late great Soviet leaders. Everything was imposing. My father was disgusted. He was disgusted when he spoke, all prideful, in Lithuanian to a man, and that man answered him back in Russian. He was disgusted to see the churches all boarded up, or turned into museums; one was an atheism museum. He didn't say anything about being disgusted, but it was all over his face.

I made a friend there; her name was Rasa. We went shopping one day; I was a desperate capitalist in need of souvenirs, which were anything but plentiful in Lithuania. Finally, I found some brooches, red pins with Lenin's face emblazoned in gold. I grabbed a handful; I would take these back to my friends. It would be sort of funny, sort of camp, sort of hip.

Rasa looked at me, horrified. "Don't do it!" she said. "Please don't take those back from my country."

That was the feeling in Lithuania, a low rumbling of dissidence. Of desperation. The countryside was beautiful, but it looked sad, worn, like it was so depressed it just wanted to sleep.

It is very hard, I think, for an American to really get this.

Eastern Europe is a land where enormous hardship has occurred; these are living memories, horrifying songs that cry out of the hillsides. It's hard for us to really contain this, to even conceive of what these people have witnessed. In 1941, about 40,000 Lithuanian people were gathered up, put in sealed boxcars and dumped, like rotten potatoes into some garbage pail, in Siberia.

And that was before the Germans came. (After the onset of World War II, the Baltic states experienced three successive occupations: first the Soviet Union, then Germany, then the Soviet Union again.)

"Some kind of machine drives up to the doors of a house, doors are opened, and music floats out," writes Riva Levy, a Lithuanian Jew now living in Israel. She has been writing the story of what happened to her life, her heart, her homeland, during the 1940s. She was young, in love. And then all hell broke loose:

> The German entices the child with sweets, candy. The mother wants to go with the child. And what is the matter with you, woman, have you lost your mind? You are not a small child . . . The doors of the machine close, the gas jets are opened, and your child will go to sleep, lulled by the music. And you, madwoman, you will stuff your clothes to make a doll—you will sing him lullabies, little songs, tell him little tales. It will be your fortune to have your hair turn white in the blink of an eye, and God will take away your mind. You are lucky, your hardships are ended. If there is no mind, there is no suffering. And what happens to your body—that is not important at all.

I've read many of Riva's tales about her life. And I've looked at her—she has a warm, knowing smile that sometimes makes her seem in charge of the whole world—and mostly what I've felt is fear. Like, "Why do you have to have these awful stories?" Erase them! I can't contain them! Do I put them in my mind, in my heart, in my soul—where? It seems I have no vacancy. Some things we can understand for only one instant at a time, before they bounce off.

Worse, we get jaded. Like, "Oh, another holocaust story." Oppression gets boring. So a little country like Lithuania isn't getting fuel now? So what? I mean, really. What's that in the grand scheme of things?

We haven't an inkling of the depths of emotion that are stirred when, having lived through Hitler, Stalin, Khrushchev, Brezhnev and the rest, a place like Lithuania says: "Enough already! Everybody just leave us alone! Let go!"

This is the ground from which their frustration swells. They look over the Baltic Sea. They sniff the cool breeze blowing down from Finland. Finland! They could have been just like Finland— free, independent, peaceful, a fair trading neighbor—if they hadn't been occupied most of the time.

And so now they're finally having their revolution. It's being called "the singing revolution." Here is a country barely the size of West Virginia, taking on one of the mega-warhead-loaded superpowers and it's doing it with . . . songs? They have initiated no violence, no bloodshed. When the Soviets were coming to occupy a building in Vilnius last April, the Lithuanians gathered around the building, held hands and sang.

When planning their independence drive, didn't they know Gorbachev would retaliate? Surely they knew. Was this a purely naive move? It seems almost like a fairy tale revolution, part Gandhi, part Martin Luther King, part Mister Rogers.

> *Yes, it is my first demonstration. Six, I am almost six. It's pretty good. Not really much fun, though. My legs get tired of standing.*
> —*Nida Degesys, Cleveland, Ohio*

The final, telling moment of my stay among the American Lithuanians in Washington didn't occur at any of the demonstrations. It happened on the way to one.

I got stopped by a cop. This was on 15th Street. We all got stopped. The cop went "TWEET" with his whistle, and we pedestrians were thus immobilized. We weren't allowed to cross the street, in any direction. "I can't cross the street?" a woman shrieked.

"Tweeet!" the cop responded.

"But I have to go to work!"

"Tweeet!"

And so we all just stood there, shaking our heads. This was not a gathering of Lithuanian Americans; these were just plain old Americans, dealing with rush hour. Many helicopters flew overhead. All the traffic was stopped. There was an eerie stillness on those streets. You could feel it on your skin: Something was about to happen.

Just then, the motorcade arrived. We all craned our necks, preparing to wave to Him. The president of the Soviet Union!

Just then, his limo stopped. In one swift motion he leaped out—it happened so fast, it was frightening, everything was out of control. This was it! He was here! He was going to . . . shake hands with the American people! The Secret Service men put their elbows out, batted down the crowd. They were big, silent, hulking. The cops were little, squirmy, loud. "Get back on the sidewalk!" they yelled, but this was a ridiculous suggestion; we were already crawling on the car.

The cops hit the people, they pushed the people, as if any of the people had a choice. It was like being caught up in a tidal wave, you had no choice where you would go. You just went forward. The people in the back wanted to get close, and so did the people behind them, and the people behind them, and so people were falling down, people were getting trampled on. "Ouch!" "Let go!" "Look out!" "Would somebody get the bike out of here!?"

"Uh, like, I really want to be here," the man with the bike said, while a woman, trying to get a picture of Gorbachev, leaned in close, too close, and one police officer got upset. "I'll run over you!" he warned, on his motorcycle. "If you don't back up I-will-run-over-you!" She didn't believe him. He revved the engine. He knocked her down.

It went on like this, all of us squished together, groping toward Gorbachev, and all you could smell was human perspiration, and just when it was clear we would not get any closer—we were jammed in as tight as we could get—and my head was smushed into the back of some lady's fleshy arm, I figured this really is a good glimpse of America's love for Gorbachev. It's a distinctive love. Kind of like the love we had for the Beatles.

When he left, the reporters took their notebooks out. They wanted to interview the people who had actually . . . shaken his hand. The news cameras clicked on. Local celebrities were born.

"It was a nice firm handshake," said Stephanie Perry, of Mount Vernon, Virginia. "It wasn't like just a little touch." The reporter was nervous.

"What do you think of Gorbachev?" he asked, shaking, vibrating so hard that Stephanie finally reached out and held his hand.

"Um, I think he's nice," she answered. "I think he is a very good president because he's, like, a really good PR man."

The reporter took her words down.

For journalists, Gorbachev's sudden stop on the street was an amazing moment to hold, caress, milk. At times like these, you don't think about things like Lithuania. Whatever really is happening in Lithuania is a side of Gorbachev few see, few even care about; we're so busy groping toward a celebrity, feeling his firm handshake. He's made Lithuania the backstage of his act, and we've obliged. Are we being duped by a showman? Maybe. Maybe not. But where are the people whose job it is to wonder?

What would I have said had I been one of the ones to speak to Gorbachev? I would, I think, not have wasted any time. I would have looked him square in the eye. I would have said: "Nyet, nyet, Soviet. Free Lithuania."

Rude, but true. That was my urge. Maybe I am a real Lithuanian after all.

After the "Gorbasm"—as I heard one man refer to it—was over, I turned my head and suddenly there was a camera aimed at my face. A man put a microphone up. He was a reporter from KYW-TV in Philadelphia. He was interviewing me. I fumbled, excused myself, said, "Wait a second," and thought how I might explain: "Hold it! I'm one of you guys. I'm not in this story!"

Or am I? I'm a journalist. I'm a Lithuanian. I'm an American. And I don't know what to do, either. The camera was rolling, and I was speechless, caught in the absurdity of the moment, this summit, this circus, where nobody seemed to hear anybody, nobody knew where to stand, and the journalists interviewed the journalists.

The Cold War has ended and everything is topsy-turvy. Perhaps the girl on the west steps of the Capitol heard the only definitive message to come out of this critical moment in history: "We-don't-know."

Branson in my Rearview Mirror   11

Just when you think you're beginning to understand America, something like Branson happens.

"Give Branson a chance," I'm thinking, turning right. I have just come out of Loretta Lynn's old theatre where Anita Bryant was singing gospel tunes and talking about when she almost committed suicide. She was in a pink dress and she had a good voice. Her hair was short.

I am driving. The Osmond Family Theatre pops up like a Pop Tart next to a Belgian Waffle House. The Ozark Mountain Buffet grabs my attention, luring me with "64 feet of good things to eat and drink." Yowza. Here comes Bobby Vinton's Blue Velvet Theatre. It is extremely . . . blue. Tony Orlando's Yellow Ribbon Music Theater is calmer. Hundreds of other drivers besides me are inching past these sights. Branson attacks you with interesting sights. John Davidson's gift shop is open at 8:30 A.M. and coffee and muffins are available, a sign says. Another announces that Andy Williams Moon River Theatre has Andy live in performance twice daily except Sunday. There is a lot of exciting neon. There are mini malls, go-cart tracks, and miniature golf courses that sit tight together and close to the road, everything squashed willy nilly into about five miles of Highway 76 as it winds through Missouri's timid Ozarks, 200 miles south of Kansas City.

I am driving. An Avis rental, teal blue, a Pontiac Grand Prix. It's funny to say, but never before have I been so emotionally attached to a car radio. I go from U2 to Mozart to B.B. King with the push of a button. These extremes provide a good counterbalance to Branson, which is extremely antiextreme. That's what draws people, I am told. People are sick of what passes for entertainment in America these days. People are sick of all the sex and violence and drugs. People are sick of being shocked. People want safety. These are the people—five million a year—who come to Branson. These are the people who put Branson second—behind Orlando, Florida—among America's most popular vacation spots to visit by car. Not only that, but these are the people who make Branson America's number one destination for buses.

Some other things you see a lot of in Branson include: bulldozers, backhoes, and men in hardhats contemplating I-beams, their large, muscular, tanned backs ready for another day of heave-hoing. Construction in Branson is a fact of life. Even Lawrence Welk is building a place in Branson, and he has been dead since 1992. The Lawrence Welk Champagne Theatre is scheduled to open soon. The folks who conceived Minnesota's Mall of America are building a giant "Heartland America" complex here—three hotels, two theatres, a shopping mall, an office complex, and miniature golf course, all under one roof. Kenny Rogers is a virtual real estate mogul in town—he just laid the keel for Branson's largest river boat theatre. Over his shoulder Kenny would be wise to keep an eye on Jimmy Osmond, the youngest one who has grown up to become the Osmond with the sharp, tycoon-type mind. Now Jimmy's involved in a project to transform 360 acres of farmland into "Branson Meadows," a faux-Victorian resort.

The construction vehicles and sheer volume of tourists turn Branson into a traffic clog from hell on most days, but anyone with a brave and pioneering spirit will soon discover that cutting through Roy Clark's parking lot will put you onto Shepherd of the Hills Expressway and give you a clear shot all the way up to Wayne Newton's Theatre. Wayne's theatre sits up high and apart from the rest, adorned by a red neon "WAYNE," 30 feet high and 70 feet long. Wayne has always thought of himself as someone who doesn't travel with the pack, a fact symbolized by the eagle pendant he wears. The only other things up near Wayne's are trees.

When you reach the outskirts of Branson, it is easy to forget civilization; you are quickly thrown into a lush and curvy landscape of lakes, mountains without scars, and secret valleys where legends of good fishing holes have echoed through the ages.

Who could have guessed it, traipsing through these hills? Who could have guessed that a segment of twentieth century America, feeling forsaken by the machinery of popular culture, would carve into these mountains a Promised Land?

There is a center turn lane on Highway 76 nobody uses unless he is actually turning, as instructed on channel 6, Branson's Vacation Channel. Everyone around here is very obedient, I'm thinking. I am late. I'm due at Roy Clark's. I'm stuck in traffic for the fourth time this day. That center turn lane sure is a big wide open lane, I'm thinking. I imagine myself just veering into that center turn lane and zooming on past these cars. But this is a useless fantasy. Things like that do not happen in Branson.

Eventually, I get to Roy's. His show stands out. It's almost uncanny. Roy's show is about . . . music. He wows you with his fiddles and nourishes you with good songs. He doesn't have a lot of fancy lights or sparkly gowns and his theatre feels more like a barn, a place you want to wear cowboy boots to. Roy's show is about as close to a bona fide concert as you'll get in Branson. Generally speaking, concerts don't work here. People get bored. Willie Nelson didn't make it in Branson when he tried in 1992, because Willie didn't put on a "show." You need a little dancing, some comedy, maybe a singing cow or something. Roy doesn't have too much of that stuff, but then again Roy was here first.

He opened his theatre back in 1983, as an investment. Nothing more. Back in those days people came to Branson basically to fish. There were a few music shows in town—the Presleys and the Baldknobbers who did hillbilly music and hillbilly humor and whose shows are still thriving. Roy's Celebrity Theatre was a place for country stars to come in and entertain the vacationers. Boxcar Willie was the first to see the light: Branson offered the opportunity for an entertainer to get off the road. Box was the first of the country singers to buy his own theatre and actually move to Branson. (Roy still lives in Oklahoma.) Then came Mickey Gilley, Ray Stevens, Moe Bandy, Mel Tillis, and pretty soon Branson became known as a country music mecca.

"To this day I have not come up with a pat answer," Roy says to me about the Branson phenomenon, the way Branson grew and what it grew into. We are back stage. He is holding a red cup. There is a chaw of tobacco tucked behind his lower lip. "Branson is something that happened," he says. "I don't think you could go out and create a Branson anywhere." He spits into the cup. "A Branson is a Branson is a Branson."

With that, Roy has handed me perhaps the most elegant answer of anybody's, and I should probably consider my search for the essence of Branson complete. But I don't. The Big Bang theory of Branson is an attractive one, but I feel compelled to seek out some more deliberate, conscious force. Surely there is logic at work here somewhere. I'm thinking about America. I'm thinking, what is the meaning of Branson and why does Branson exist?

I decide to ask Tony Orlando.

"IS THIS A MIRACLE OR WHAT!?" Tony says. I am now sitting in his $9 million theatre, backstage in the apartment he built so he can rest between shows. He is so happy to be in Branson that it's hard to get a word in edgewise. "It's a miracle," he says. He is looking, well, older than the Tony Orlando I remember on TV with Dawn, and beefier. He is welcoming, generous, and so very happy to be alive that it begins to rub off.

Tony was part of Branson's second wave of immigration. Following the country music stars were the ex-TV stars and lounge acts (Andy Williams, John Davidson, the Osmond family, Bobby Vinton, Wayne Newton), who also built theatres and moved here. They figured they could offer Branson's vacationers the same kind of entertainment that the country stars were putting out. Good, wholesome family entertainment. You hear those words a lot around here. There are no dirty jokes told in Branson. No alcohol in the theatres. No strip joints anywhere near the town. No porno shops. None of that bad stuff. Just good, whole- some family entertainment.

"This is the heartland of America!" Tony says to me. "Look at Branson on the map. If the United States had a heart and it were a living and breathing animal, Branson would be right where the heart is. Take a look at it! Put that in your article! Maybe there's an energy. Maybe there's a pull to the center of all things. Maybe there really is."

Tony is a passionate metaphor machine. "If you could put a wall around Branson, you'd have Disneyland," he says. "I'm like

'The Pirates of the Caribbean.' Some other entertainer is 'Thunder Mountain.' And someone else is 'The Haunted House.' We are all rides within this little town that has a Disneyesque feeling. And my job is to do that ride that makes those kids smile."

The Disneyland analogy is especially useful when you note where it breaks down. Disneyland is a fantasy, a place you know is fake and enter with the understanding that it will be a respite from the real world.

Branson, on the other hand, is the real world.

People come to Branson from all over America, although most seem to roll in from points not far away in the midwest. Typically, they see two shows a day. There are 34 theatres to choose from, almost all with 3 P.M. and 8 P.M. performances. Tickets are affordable: about $16.

You get to the show early to browse in the gift shop that each star has. You peruse the selection of John Davidson special-blend teas, for example, or note that the Osmond Family Caramel Corn looks suspiciously like the Wayne Newton Caramel Corn and the Tony Orlando Caramel Corn, but no matter. Bobby Vinton has jams and jellies. The show begins. The theatres are big, new, and the lighting and sound systems are state-of-the-art. Most of the shows have the same basic format: You get a little dancing, some sing-alongs, pretty gals in sparkly gowns, a few Hillary Clinton jokes, intermission, popcorn, soft drink in a souvenir cup, then more jokes, songs about God followed by an intensely patriotic finale during which people in the audience stand up and cry. The 3 P.M. show ends precisely at 5 P.M. No encore. No real exuberant chatting among the audience as they file out, quickly, to the buses. Everybody eats dinner in time to make it to the next show, down the road, at 8. Then it's gift shop, sing-along, sparkly gowns,

Hillary jokes, intermission, popcorn, soft drink, souvenir cup, God, country, tears. This show ends precisely at 10. Everybody is tucked into their motel room beds by 11, when Highway 76 becomes so quiet some people say you could go out and shoot deer. Nobody gets drunk. Nobody gets offended. Everything is clean and nobody gets hurt.

I visit the Osmonds and they explain everything to me. There are a lot of Osmonds here. Approximately 38, in fact, including Mom and Dad Osmond, all of whom left Utah and settled in Branson in 1992. (Donny shows up on special occassions. Marie comes by more often.) The family is committed to this town because, they tell me, Branson is a place to which people come not just to hear music but to confirm their convictions about America and God.

The lobby of their theatre is sort of like an Osmond museum. The walls are covered with pictures and memorabilia of the Osmonds from the old days. Over the right door into the theatre is a portrait of George and Barbara Bush and over the left is a portrait of Ronald and Nancy Reagan. There are celebrity pictures all over the place.

Merrill, Alan, Jay and Wayne Osmond sit with me in the lobby and tell me Branson is an oasis. America, one or another Osmond points out, "is going down the toilet." Branson is moral majority land, they say, explaining that Branson is about the good people of this earth coming together and celebrating the good things of this earth: love, peace, and family.

"I'm trying to understand what you mean specifically . . ." I keep saying. Who are the good people and what are their names? We talk late into the night. I appreciate the generosity and passion of these men, but I don't understand their version of how the world is divided. They talk of "love" and "peace," as if these were objects, the stuff of their Moral Majority Land that simply does not exist out here in Amoral Minority Land. Which I am, by default, part of. The Osmonds seem to think that the people where I come from regard love and peace as stupid and repulsive things that must be stamped out or something. I really don't understand. "It all comes down to family values," they say. "What is a family value?" I ask, and we go off on a discussion about what made America great and how the media are undoing God's work and sucking us all down the aforementioned toilet. Eventually, teenagers come out with vacuum cleaners and encircle us with noise.

"We came to this earth with free agency," Merrill Osmond concludes. "The problem is, we don't have enough role models that have the basics figured out that can preach to the masses the correct way."

Branson, I am told, embodies the correct way.

It's funny to say, but I've never before been drawn to Nirvana. Now all of a sudden I have Nirvana on the radio, turned up loud. Something about the angry howls of youth feels refreshing. Maybe it's the "us" and "them" division that I sense developing as I explore Branson. The deeper I go the more I feel like an outsider, part of the bad world, a dirty blotch on the landscape of this, the good world.

Where I am presently stuck in traffic. I'm always stuck in traffic. I can't stand it anymore. I pull off the road and walk. I drop by Shoji Tabuchi's place. Nobody really argues the point that the fanciest theatre in town is Shoji Tabuchi's. Shoji is a Japanese violinist who is commonly referred to as the American dream come true. He came to this country 20 years ago with $500 in his pocket and another $100 in his shoe, the myth goes. People say he is a living example of what can happen to you in America if you just apply yourself.

Shoji's theatre is purple, and the entire front is outlined in neon. Shoji's name appears spelled out in flashing lights that go in sequence, S-H-O-J-I, and perched above that is a giant picture of Shoji with his beautiful blonde American wife. The lobby is packed most hours of most days with people absorbing the opulence. The bathrooms are so fancy you can buy postcard pictures of them in the gift shop. "Seems to me there's more lookers than goers," says one woman who actually wants to *use* the bathroom. The line for the ladies room snakes around the lobby, all the women with cameras out and ready. The men's room has a pool table in it. "Now George, I want you to go in there and memorize *everything*," a woman is saying to her husband. "Yeah," says George. He emerges a few minutes later with a look of horror on his face.

"Well . . .?" the wife says.

"A little too fancy for my tastes," says George.

"Duh," the wife says, giving her husband a look of exhaustion and disgust. "It-is-not-supposed-to-be-for-your-tastes-George. It's supposed to be spectacular!"

Anyway, Shoji's place sure is fancy, I'm thinking, and I go outside and continue my walk. Eventually, I get up to Ray Stevens's place. He and I get into a discussion about dirty jokes. You just don't tell dirty jokes in Branson, he is saying. You will get run out of town. When Wayne Newton first came to Branson he put on a benefit for the College of the Ozarks and raised several thousand dollars. But Wayne had curse words and other racy things in his show and so the college did not accept the money.

Ray tells me that America is moving away from off color humor anyway; the dirty joke period was just an adolescent phase we went through. "We were just pinching our pimples," he says. "The more sophisticated an audience gets the more they see through the obvious dirty jokes. It's shooting ducks in a barrel, you know? Why do it?"

I go to see Ray's show, the most popular in town. Ray sells out 2,000 seats, twice a day, six days a week. There are a lot of fat lady and bald man jokes. The people around me are laughing so hard some of them are crying. There is Elvis coming down in a UFO and some pink aliens running around. There are entire songs done in chicken clucks. There is a lot of zany stuff. "I have nine kids," one of the characters on stage says. "I was going to have another until I heard that every tenth child born in America is Hispanic." Ha ha ha. Hispanic. Get it? No? Well, this is very sophisticated humor.

It reminds me of the juggler I saw during Andy Williams's show. He did a clever skit about Adam and Eve, wearing different hats to indicate characters. When it got to the part about the devil tempting Eve with the apple, the juggler put on an afro wig and held a boom box and sang a rap song. Well, it wasn't exactly supposed to be a joke that the devil was a black man. It was more a natural type thing.

Good wholesome family entertainment.

I take a break from seeing shows and just drive around for an afternoon with my radio, feeling safe in my bad-world cocoon. I get out of town and explore the countryside. I get out of the Pontiac and touch the ground. I take my shoes off and dip my toes in Table Rock Lake. I breathe the air. I lie back and shut my eyes.

Just then, a monstrous white amphibious vehicle loaded with innocent senior citizens comes out of the lake and nearly runs me over.

It is not a dream.

Forget it. I go back to town and sit in traffic. I abandon my car yet again and walk. I end up at the "WAX and historical MUSEUM." This turns out to be my favorite place in Branson.

It is perhaps Branson's truest house of art. Indigenous art, mind you. The kind of art that is so removed from any self conscious desire for greatness that it stands as a pure reflection of the soul of a culture.

You pay $2 and the cashier hands you a token. You walk two feet, put the token into a turnstile, and enter. There is: wood paneling, a low ceiling, a smell of mildew, dripping air conditioners, a '48 Chrysler, a '37 Packard. A taxidermy display featuring a two-headed calf. The '61 Cadillac Jacqueline Kennedy rode to President Kennedy's funeral in. Jacqueline is in there, a black veil over her head. The car is missing a windshield wiper. A Kennedy portrait on black velvet hangs above a plastic plant. On the opposite wall is an arrowhead collection. You are just getting started.

In wax, behind Plexiglas, appear Mary Pickford, Gary Cooper, Marlene Dietrich with mildew on her dress. Everything is old. Everything is dusty. There are Charlie Chaplin, Charles Lindberg, Jean Harlowe in bed with a stuffed cat. Elvis is given perhaps the most prominence. I know this because almost every hallway I turn down affords an Elvis view. The halls are narrow, dark, musty; light bulbs stick out of panelling; the floor is creaky, the carpet is barely carpet anymore. There are Marlin (sic) Brando, and the creator of the Kewpie doll, a 1923 Dodge, whoops, Betsy Ross, George Washington, John Travolta, Mahatma Gandi (sic), Bela Lugosi, Mark Twain, Nazis in coffins, Hitler, Eva Braun, and a "top Nazi crook" followed by Benito Mussolini as he actually appeared just before burial in a secret grave, bloated, with holes all over him and blood spurting out. Elvis. Ronald Reagan looking on, Oliver North at his feet.

And there is Dolly Parton just exploding out of that dress with Burt Reynolds not even noticing. More mildew, Thomas Edison, more taxidermy delights, Moses, and finally, Jesus. Jesus illuminated by black lights. Jesus turning water into wine. Elvis. Jesus in a Last Supper scene with grapes and pita bread on his plate and everyone, including Jesus, has a place card, mildew, air conditioners with duct tape, and you exit as if from a tunnel of tragedy to a sunny room with t-shirts and mugs for sale.

Ron Waggoner, the manager, tells me the WAX and historical MUSEUM started out in Oklahoma, traveled to Florida, and ended up settling in Branson more than 20 years ago. It consists of 17 house trailers strung together. It is the work of C.C. Long, now deceased. It is his lifetime collection of stuff. The family has tried to keep the business up and last year wanted to buy a wax Schwarzkopf but he cost $5,000. Marilyn Monroe cost $3,800. Dolly Parton and Burt Reynolds came as a set. When you buy a wax figure all you get is the head and sometimes the hands. You have to build the body yourself and sometimes even put on the hair.

Then Ron tells me the news: the WAX and historical MUSEUM is about to close down. A foreign investor has come in and bought up this land and has decided to remove this place and build a Shirt Shack.

"It is sad," says Ron. But he is philosophical. This is Branson's future. "In Branson, the mom and pop thing is dead."

Ron is not a Branson native. He came here, like a lot of people, five years ago when the word got out that Branson was a boom town. Originally from western Iowa, Ron did not take easily to Branson life.

"Well, I had never even heard the term 'sand nigger' before," he says. "I kept hearing them talk about the sand niggers, and I'm thinking, 'what?' I guess sand niggers include Pakistanis, Iranians, the desert type people. I bet it took me three months to catch on to that one. I'm not a fast learner."

Ron educates me. Other people not tolerated down here include: blacks, Jews, homosexuals, east coast people and your new age types. He points out that there are virtually no black people living anywhere near Branson. Homosexuals? "Oh, forget that, oh jeez, you don't even mention that." East coast people are "just a different breed," and new agers are basically pagans from hell. "You get anything off the Bible and people here kind of go into a tizzy," says Ron. "In this town you are a Baptist and a Republican, or you are nothing. And of course I'm a Presbyterian and a Democrat, so. Plus I've been to the new age book store a couple of times, so I'm a weirdo from way back, I'm sure.

"People here have one idea and they follow it and there's no jogging it one way or the other. If you don't believe the way they do they don't trust you. It's just bitter, bitter, bitter people."

I buy a t-shirt from Ron and a mug.

The funny thing I'm noticing is I'm beginning to get the urge to act out. Maybe it's the traffic. Maybe it's the foul smell of bigotry. Maybe it's my own frustration at trying to figure out what a family value is if not the willingness to embrace all of humankind into one happy family regardless of race, creed or color. Duh. How totally naive. I almost sound patriotic or something. I am stuck outside Jim Stafford's theatre. Nobody is moving. Oh, come on. I want to beep my horn. It occurs to me that my whole time in Branson I have heard not one horn. Everybody is patient. Everybody is cheerful. Everybody is safe. This is the good world. The heck with the horn, I think, I want to turn into that forbidden center turn lane and make a getaway past all these cars. Just zoom on away. But everyone is so complacent and happy. I can't do it.

Instead, I make a U-turn, angle through Roy Clark's parking lot, and find that shortcut on to Shepherd of the Hills Expressway. The road is clear and I zoom, just to remember what zooming feels like.

I'm thinking of Wayne Newton, the first entertainer I talked to when I got to Branson. I am missing Wayne. Everything was so simple with Wayne. He didn't make any big claims about God or America; he was just Wayne. The king of Vegas, Wayne was getting disillusioned with Vegas. Wayne thought Vegas was changing into a place he could hardly recognize—what with all that family entertainment coming in, those stupid theme parks and rides— so he was looking for alternatives. He decided to split his time between Vegas and Branson. Branson, to Wayne, could become the Vegas he once knew, a place where the entertainer rules. Wayne even went way out on a limb and said he thought gambling would one day be here in Branson. Gambling wouldn't hurt anybody, Wayne said defensively. He had, after all, as a single parent raised his beloved daughter in the gambling capitol of America, and his daughter had turned into a fine, creative, beautiful, intelligent young woman, thank you very much, said Wayne.

Everybody in Branson knows how Wayne feels about gambling. And nobody agrees. Everybody knows what gambling is: the essence of evil. The stuff that must never be allowed to infiltrate the mythical walls of Branson. There is so much bad stuff out there in the bad world.

I am zooming. I am thinking about evil. I am thinking about the mayor of Branson, Wade Meadows. He told me about the "bad element." Along with your tourists comes your bad element, he said. He was not happy about what was happening to Branson— and not just because of the sewer problem, although that certainly is a problem. Five million visitors a year definitely presents a challenge to a sewer plant built for 3,700, which is technically the population of Branson. "You know, full is full," the mayor said.

But the other problem is the bad element. Pretty soon there will be homeless coming in here, the mayor said. Branson never really had the bad element before.

Even shoplifting was now in Branson, he said. "I guess the more the people come here, the more the shoplifters come, too." The shoplifters, like the homeless, weren't included in the "people" category. These were objects, dirty things invented by God for reasons nobody could totally ascertain.

So, the outside world. My world. According to Branson mythology, America has indeed turned into a disgusting place. It is a land of satanic rap music, murder, driveby shootings, moral decay, Beavis and Butt-head, and other evils embraced by Hillary Clinton. Not so much her husband. He is too stupid to bother worrying about. Hillary, and people like her, are all those folks out there with no family values.

It all comes down to family values. Like shoplifters and the homeless, like love and like peace, family values are talked about as objects. It is never said where these things are available or how you get them. Everybody just seems to know.

I end up at the home of Branson's only psychic. I'd heard about her. In an editorial in a Branson newspaper, a writer talked about the evil force infiltrating Branson and offered as proof the fact that Branson now had a psychic living within its borders.

The psychic won't talk to me, won't give me her name, doesn't want to make waves against "them." She calls them "the Bible belt people."

"Don't listen to them," she says. "They will just corrupt your mind. There's only 3,000 of them in this town. There's more of us. We will win." She says goodbye. She says don't use her name. She says stay away from here.

I get back to my car only to discover that my car radio is dead. Jeezus! My radio! I am cut off. I am alone. I wonder if the psychic did it. I wonder if the Bible belt people did it. I keep trying the radio. Nothing. Things just get weirder and weirder from this point on.

Maybe the tape player works. I go to the mall. In Consumer's, the food store, I see a selection of tapes for $4.99 each. Not a very large selection. Eventually, I choose Bob Marley. At the cash register, the teenager starts laughing. "Check it out!" he says to the bagger next to him. "Bob Marley! Bob Marley in Branson!"

"Bob Marley is dead," the bagger says.

"Dude," says the cashier, "so is Lawrence Welk."

I begin to seriously wonder what it would be like to be a teenager growing up in Branson.

Beyond Consumer's is Wal-Mart and in between is the mall. Donny Sneed is playing the mall. He has a very good voice for a mall act. I sit and listen. Afterwards, I talk to him. He is happy, like Tony Orlando, despite the fact that his career isn't going quite as gangbusters as Tony's. "Well, it's difficult to come to Branson and just jump into a theatre, so you do what you have to do."

He tells me living in Branson is difficult for a lot of people. "The average working guy can't afford to live anywhere near town because everybody that's got a dump worth $250 is getting $500 for it." He tells me a Vegas outfit is opening a theatre at the mall and so the mall has told Donny he will be officially out of a job at the end of the month. "I don't know where I will go," he says.

I notice he is taking up a collection, the first I've seen, for Branson's flood victims. "These people are desperate," he tells me, explaining that the disaster in the flood plains up north hurt tourism down here pretty bad and so nobody is too eager to publicize what happened lately in Branson. About a week ago a storm came and engulfed a couple of trailer parks down near Bull Creek.

In the car, I put the Bob Marley tape in. It works. "Lively Up Yourself," I sing, and head down to the Linda Vista trailer park. Not trailers, these are "mobiles," I am told. Sorry. Twelve mobiles just up and floated down Bull Creek and never were found. About 150 others floated around and banged into one other and some landed on top of others, and when the water finally went away all that was left was a smelly mess of collided homes and a lot of flies.

Many of the people who live in the mobile home parks are the musicians and ushers and snack bar ladies who work in the theatres. You can't afford to live in town in Branson anymore.

Sitting by her destroyed mobile, an elderly woman starts crying. "Them big shot entertainers has got the money and they need us little people to make their money but they don't want to hand it down to us," she says.

Everybody is complaining that the rich fat cat entertainers aren't doing anything to help the little people in their hour of need. And yet these people are all wearing t-shirts that Mel Tillis just brought down yesterday. John Davidson was recently down here and so was Tony Orlando. In fact, thousands of dollars have come into the Red Cross from relief efforts run by the entertainers. Boxcar Willie alone raised $13,800 for the flood victims.

But they gave the money to the Red Cross. These people don't trust the Red Cross. The Red Cross is just part of the bureaucratic world they hate. And what is the Red Cross doing? Giving them temporary housing, clothes, supplies, and three hot meals a day. "Big whup," I'm told. "They're wasting the money," says one woman. "Like last night for dinner we had half a barbecue chicken and three ribs, plus roll, plus potato salad, plus beans, you know, which is ridiculous. People don't need that much to eat."

"What we need is money," says another.

"Just give us cash," says another.

"Someone please help us!" says another.

Feeling confused, feeling dirty, wondering if I am now in the good world or the bad world, I reach into my pocket and pull out a 20. I hand it over. I have to leave. I am due at John Davidson's. I crawl back through town. John Davidson is tall. His hair is huge. His voice is enormous. He says Branson has given him the opportunity to revive his art. "I am in the prime of my show," he says. I ask him about the flood victims and tell him that the people appreciated the fact that he came down to look around. "It's so sad," he says. "Some of those people lost everything.

"But then again you have to say, well, why do they live in a creekbed? You know, it's like, duh."

I sit through John Davidson's show, eating popcorn, sipping Diet Coke out of my John Davidson souvenir cup. John is singing about how great America is, and he is wearing a red, white and blue jacket with fringe and sequins and there are slides on either side of him from when he was the host of *Hollywood Squares.*

It's funny, but I believe I am about to hyperventilate. I never hyperventilated before.

Finally, I relax, feeling stupid. Duh. I realize where I am. Here I thought I had actually left the WAX and historical MUSEUM. But I think I may be lost in that creepy, miscellaneous place. Now that's a good metaphor. Branson is a museum. Branson doesn't mean anything. A Branson is a Branson is a WAX and historical MUSEUM. Branson is art. Indigenous art, mind you. The kind of art that is so removed from any self-conscious desire for greatness that it stands as a pure reflection of the soul of a culture. If

Branson were a painting on a wall, people would look at it, cock their heads, and say, "What whimsy! How very vital! A chilling depiction of the paradox of American patriotism." This is a lot of entertainment for $2, I think. They shouldn't make it into a Shirt Shack.

I leave John Davidson's, crank up Bob Marley, and do it. I go speeding down the forbidden center turn lane, zoom all the way down past Bobby Vinton's, and shout "Yee Hoo," like a demonic crazy lady.

God Bless America.

Cats | **12**

I got a cat. I called him: Bob. We were having a good life. I didn't want any more cats, but then a little gray stray came along and bulldozed his way into my heart, and so I became a two-cat person. For a long time I couldn't figure out the name of this second cat. Then one day I looked at him and realized his name was: Steve. Now another cat is coming around. I don't want a third cat. When you become a three-cat person, you join a separate class. This class includes eight-cat people and 20-cat people and those interesting ladies with 600 or so cats you hear about on the news.

I am thinking these things, up at 3:30 A.M., unable to sleep. Maybe everybody has those nights when the mind seizes. Your attention clamps down on a subject and no matter how hard you try you can't release it. It can be a serious subject. Maybe you're worried about a big crime you committed, or maybe you're noting some inner ache of loneliness. Or it can be a seemingly meaningless and stupid subject that isn't going to affect your destiny or anybody else's. My situation is in that last category.

What awoke me from a sound sleep tonight was the image of Socks, Chelsea Clinton's cat.

Earlier today I came across a picture of Socks in a magazine that ran photographs of 1992. These were the images of last year, the magazine suggested, and so there were the faces of starving people in Somalia, scenes of the Los Angeles riots, portraits of an exasperated Princess Di and a fed-up Prince Charles. And then the last picture, a full page leading us into 1993, was that picture of Socks. The picture that will go down in history as an artifact of our times. The picture of a throng of beefy photographers stalking Socks outside the governor's mansion in Arkansas last November. Socks is looking out at all of us, ears bent back, appearing anxious. "Who are these fools?" he seems to say. Or, "How did my life get so complicated?" Or, simply, "Help." I keep seeing that picture in my head and I keep thinking: that poor cat.

The Humane Society of the United States, the American Society for the Prevention of Cruelty to Animals, and some other animal groups got together and named 1993 the Year of the Cat. Cats are on people's minds, thanks to Socks. The last cat in the White House was Misty Malarky Ying Yang, Amy Carter's Siamese. And before that there was Shan, Gerald Ford's cat. Ronald Reagan was the one who switched the place over to dogs, first with Lucky, then Rex. And then, of course, came Millie, perhaps the only dog with an income big enough ($890,000 in royalties from her first book) to win the respect of stockbrokers.

Looking back, you see that a lot of presidents were cat people. Calvin Coolidge had two cats, one of which reportedly worked part time as an elevator attendant. Theodore Roosevelt had a six-toed cat called Slippers. George Washington, Thomas Jefferson, Abraham Lincoln, Rutherford B. Hayes, Herbert Hoover and John Kennedy all owned cats while they were in the

White House. I don't suppose any of those cats became as famous as Socks already is, and I do suppose this is a sign of our times. Those presidents didn't have wars you could watch on TV either. Those presidents all lived in a time before the media conquered the world.

Anyway, with Socks in the White House, will cat people be to the 1990s what dog people were to the 1980s? Well, I don't know. For one thing, I don't think it follows that just because you're pro-cat you're anti-dog. I know I'm not. But still, you have to admit that cat people are a distinct breed of people.

It's good to stay up all night and figure things like this out sometimes.

Bob, my cat, is now on my legs. I knew this would happen. Bob is in love with me. Bob is thrilled that I am awake and down here on the living room couch, instead of upstairs hidden behind my bedroom door. Bob is a somewhat gigantic orange barn cat, about 8 years old, and very tall for a cat. When people first see Bob they usually say, "My, what a large cat." I tell them Bob played football in college.

I give Bob a few strokes between the ears and hear his purring start. This purring gets embarrassingly loud sometimes; inevitably Bob begins sounding like he's got a jackhammer in him working on his throat bones. Bob is not self-conscious like most cats. Bob is not cool. Bob, I think, wouldn't mind being a dog.

Bob drools when he is happy, as if unable to contain all his joy and so allowing it to flow freely forth. Mostly, Bob feels this happiness any moment he is sitting near or on me. Bob follows me around the house when I clean, and through the city streets when I take walks. Sometimes when I sit down he sits down in front of me, and stares at me, his head slightly cocked, his eyes wearing a look of unreasonable satisfaction. "Bob!" I'll say. "Go catch a mole! Go roll over a ball of yarn! Go, Bob. Go be a cat!"

But Bob will say nothing. Bob just stares at me with his glare of adoration and devotion. Bob has always been in love with me and I'm afraid Bob always will be.

"Good night, Bob," I say. I close my eyes and try to get this sleeping situation underway. I see: Socks again. Then I see: Meg Ryan, the actress. Insomnia makes your mind go funny like this. I was, in fact, supposed to go interview Meg Ryan for a magazine article but then at the last minute "her people" canceled. Well, they canceled me. They had read some of my other stories and they said one of them, a story about Susan Sarandon, was too "snippy." "Snippy?" I thought. I was not conscious of any snippiness in my mood at the time of writing it. But that's the way it works in celebrity journalism nowadays. You give your voice away to the publicists or else the publicists kick your voice out from under you.

Cats are more interesting than Meg Ryan's people, when you get right down to it. Cats could care less what you say about them or their people. Cats rule. Cats, like all nonhumans you get to know, keep you human.

How does a person become a cat person? Looking back, you can usually figure it all out.

As a kid I was a crusader for the eternal life of all animals. I blessed myself. In the name of the Father and of the Son and of the Holy Spirit, I motioned, every single time I saw a dead animal. It didn't matter what kind. Usually it was just some disgusting road-kill. I figured someone had better start sending the animals to Heaven. The subject of animal afterlife was, after all, never—not once—mentioned in church. Where I got the power to send an animal to Heaven is not something I can say for sure.

My animal-soul rescue service began, I think, right about the time my cat Jinx got hit by a car and died. Everybody has a first pet death story, and mine is pretty typical, I guess. Jinx was an ordinary fussy shorthair whom I befriended when I was quite young. One morning I awoke to hear my sister sobbing. My mother was consoling her, relating the story of when her first pet, a parakeet, died. My mother, who is not a cat person or any other animal person, apparently never quite got over the parakeet situation. Her feeling about pets is: Don't get them because they just die. Life deals you enough abandonment with people; you don't need to add to the trouble with pets.

I figured Jinx had died. I figured right. For a long time I looked at the spot out on our street where the car had hit her. I concluded, based on zero evidence, that the killer was the teenager next door who did it with his recklessness. I vowed right then and there never to become a teenager. I would stay a kid and I would crusade for dead animals. This became my life's work.

And so. And so after Jinx got murdered by that evil teenager, my dad took me out to get a new cat. We found one that looked exactly like Jinx. And we named it: Jinx. How's that for denial? One interesting thing about Bill and Hillary Clinton is that they did not do this. Their decision when Chelsea's dog, Zeke, died a few years ago was to not get Chelsea another dog. Allow her time to grieve over the dog, the reasoning supposedly went. That may indeed have been a Good Parenting Moment. Even though Bill and Hillary are allergic to cats, they elected to get Chelsea a cat to replace Zeke. This is how Socks came to be. Little did Socks know what the world had in store for him. *People* magazine has already run several features on Socks, including an interview with a cat psychologist who speculated about Socks's mental health, now that he has been propelled without his consent to superstardom. Socks's first cover story was in *Cats Magazine* in January. *Media Week* claims to have had the first-ever interview with Socks. During the inauguration there was a giant Socks float, and Washington bakeries have started selling cookies in the shape of Socks. In cities all across America it is happening. People are entering contests to see who can draw a portrait that best depicts Socks. Cat shops that specialize in cat knickknacks are running out of black and white cat coffee mugs, black and white cat doorstops, and black and white cat ceramic figurines.

And I am not one to talk. I am up with insomnia, thinking about Socks.

My cat Jinx was black and white.

If there was ever any doubt that I was to become a cat person, my experience with the second Jinx, the reincarnated Jinx, certainly sealed the deal.

We got along famously. In fact, "Jinx" became my nickname. We were Jinx and Jinx, best friends. I was the youngest of four kids and Jinx was the only being I knew who was younger than me. She was the only one I could boss around, take care of, feel larger than. Jinx and I bonded. For Halloween I would dress up as: Jinx. I would tell Jinx during sleepless nights that she was the only one in the family who understood me. The rest of them were crazy. It was Jinx and Jinx against the world.

Years went by. We moved into a fancy rich-person house. Jinx couldn't deal with the transition. Jinx went nuts. She tore up the new furniture. She forgot how to use a litter box. She tore up the new drapes. She attacked the Oriental rugs. She had a glazed look in her eyes, a monster not quite sure what to ruin next. I became very worried about her mental health, while my mother—not, I remind you, a cat person—became concerned about her own. This lunatic beast was tearing up my mother's dream home.

One day, I couldn't find the cat. Where's the cat? Three days went by and I was still calling and calling outside for the cat. Eventually, I figured it out. I confronted my parents. They said,

"Yes." I could see—thank God—the regret in their eyes. I could see in their eyes the admission that this might truly have been one astoundingly Bad Parenting Moment. Well, it was a choice. They apologized. I couldn't even talk to them. I ran out the door. I hopped on my bike and pedaled like a maniac to the SPCA. Did they still have Jinx? No, Jinx had already been sent into "the other room."

Jinx had been murdered. My own parents had sent my best friend to the gas chamber. I could not accept this fact. I needed to throw up. I did. I got back on my bike and rode through the wind with tears coming down my face that stung and sizzled and couldn't begin to cool down the heat of my wild child despair. I held the handlebar with just my left hand, leaving my right hand free to bless myself over and over and over again, frantically, sending Jinx and hundreds of other animals to Heaven that day.

I am at this point beginning to become conscious of some snippiness in my mood. This night is just not cooperating. This night has a life all its own. The furnace is talking to the refrigerator and now the clock is interrupting with its own questions. Shut up, everybody. I'm getting angry. I'm getting tense. I'm demanding sleep, thereby ensuring I will get none. It's maddening to have cats around at a time like this. Cats specialize in sleep and you just look at them all curled up and peaceful and you get totally jealous.

Steve, my aforementioned second cat, is stretched out over there on top of the radiator. Steve likes me okay, but Steve does not drool over the sight of me like Bob does. Steve knows not to come too close to me when Bob is around. Steve waits till the coast is clear.

I pick up a cat book. Domestic cats have been around since

1700 B.C. They came from Egypt. A lot of cats have the Nefertiti look, when you think about it. Fifty percent of all the homes in America are now peopled with cats. Cats are jewels, to some people. They are sleek, luxurious, pretty adornments for the home. To other people they are low maintenance companions. Houseplants that purr and move into the sun on their own. Then again, for a lot of other people, cats are creatures of intrigue because you can never quite figure out a cat. The only thing you can train a cat to do is: nothing. Cats are really good at doing nothing, which sounds easy but isn't; you achieve nothingness only when you embrace everythingness. Cats understand. Cats, I think, are Buddhists. Cats are aloof. Cats are mavericks. You can't catch a cat and make him love you. If a cat hops onto your lap, you feel chosen. "He picked me!" Cats are blind dates you actually end up liking and worry whether they'll ever call again. But a cat will call you only when he's good and ready.

Except, I tell you, for Bob.

At this point Bob has his wet nose implanted in my neck. I knew this would happen. The purring is going on so loud I can feel it in my teeth. This is why I can't have Bob in my room at night. If it were up to Bob, we would spend every night with him sleeping on my face.

"Bob!" I say. "Move over!" But Bob says nothing. He just keeps humming his tune of devotion and adoration. Sometimes I have a hard time believing that this Bob is the same as the other Bob that Bob sometimes turns into.

Bob, you understand, is violent. Bob is a soldier. And not just any soldier. Bob is a Marine. It is shocking to see him go from tender loving cat to . . . Ram-bob. But he does. If another cat comes into the yard, Bob will not wait, sniff or in any other way stop to assess the situation. Bob will simply rip the other cat's face off. And he's good at it. He's swift. He's a hunter. If he's hungry and does not like the flavor of Nine Lives I have provided him, he will step outside, look around, and take one great swipe into the air and pull a bird down. He will eat this bird, head and all. And then he will come back inside to resume adoring me. "That's disgusting, Bob," I'll say.

But Bob will say nothing.

You can imagine, then, the battlefield my home turned into when Steve entered my life. Steve was a homeless cat, a non-descript runt, gray and brown striped, dirty and grimy. He was a kitten who had made a home in my window well one fall, and to this day I don't know why Bob permitted even this. The kitten stayed in the window well until the temperature dipped below 30. Then he howled. He stood at the back door and howled for hours that turned into days. He demanded entry. This, he decided, would be his home and Bob and I were to have little say in the matter.

Eventually, he became: Steve. Eventually, he became hand-some. Eventually, this wild cat grew sweet and calm and joined our family. It was at this point that Bob became thirsty for Steve's blood.

For about a year, I suppose, the war went on. Sometimes Steve would be sound asleep, just snoozing away, and Bob would awake him with a great toothy lunge at his face. Bob would chew Steve up. And Steve was just a little runt. And Bob was Rambob. And I would have to intervene. I would scream and yell at Bob for being such a big fat brute (Bad Parenting Moment), and then I would have to go catch Steve and comfort him. And the sight of this would just sicken Bob, and quadruple Bob's rage. And then I'd have to take both of them to the vet because the puncture wounds caused big disgusting abscesses that blew up on their necks and legs. And Bob would howl like a wolf the whole way to the vet, and Steve—every single time I took Steve to the vet, Steve would wet his pants. And one time Bob went number two in his cat carrier and just by coincidence the driver in front of me slammed on his brakes, and so I slammed on my brakes, and Bob went rolling and rolling and rolling in the cat carrier with the number two in it, all around the back of the car, and when I pulled over and took him out he looked up at me, exhausted and limp, like, this is the worst day of my entire life. And then Steve regressed, letting out some of his old alien cat growls, and we were on a highway, and trucks were zooming by, terrifying Bob, terrifying Steve, terrifying me, and I didn't know where to put Bob, or the soiled cat carrier, or where to turn next.

Sooner or later you think: Why am I doing this? I have a life. I have friends. I have a job. Heck, I know Susan Sarandon. I know Tom Cruise. I know Mel Gibson. I almost know Meg Ryan. I know Axl Rose and I even know Geraldo. Why aren't I off wearing sparkly gowns and drinking champagne with the rich and famous? Why am I spending all this time nursing and loving and rearing two fighting cats?

It isn't a matter of choosing. When you are a cat person you need a cat just like you need a house and you need clothes. It's a matter of repetition. After a certain age every relationship you have becomes a duplication. You've been here before, know the deal; this whole thing is an echo of something that once was. It is likely that if you had a primary relationship with a cat when you were young, you will always need a cat in your life.

Cats, in the end, help you focus. Cats bring you out of the made-up world of celebrities and publicists, presidents, taxes, bills to pay, appointments to keep, and all the things that make sense only in the light of day. Cats bring you into the night, into the real world of ear mites and puncture wounds, dead birds and howling toms, violation, war, and forgiveness.

Bob eventually let up on Steve. And because Steve stuck out

those days of violent attacks, Bob got his first and only cat companion. Lately, the two have spent a lot of time playing hide-and-seek. Bob will peek around a chair at Steve, then retreat. Bob's whole body will vibrate, getting ready to pounce, but then suddenly there will be Steve, having zipped around from the other side of the chair, shocking the pants off Bob. They'll look at each other, wide-eyed and jaws slightly ajar, which is about as close as cats get to laughing, I think.

And so. And so dawn is just about here. The sun is not coming through loud and clear yet, but I can hear the birds outside starting to discuss the day's plans. And I never got back to sleep. And I never got over the loss of Jinx. And I feel a lot better. It's always better to move through, instead of over, a loss. I guess that's why Socks woke me up in the first place. Socks is an inkblot, just like Meg Ryan and all the other celebrities. We project onto them our own weakness and powerfulness, hopefulness and helplessness, darkness and lightness, blackness and whiteness of being.

Tom Cruise | **13**

All the women here call him Tom, and all the men call him Cruise. Get hip. Move along. Don't ask questions. We're in Daytona Beach, Florida, where the Paramount people are working like maniacs in this thick humidity trying to get the movie *Days of Thunder* done. Time is running out. The weather is not cooperating. Everybody's tense. There really is no time for this frivolity, but Cruise is keeping his word. His press agent and the estimated 4,000 other dragon ladies who surround and protect him (that number could be an exaggeration on my part) have arranged for him to take me for a spin around the Daytona International Speedway.

He arrives. He's dressed in a one-piece racing suit, black and lime green, zipped down so the top half hangs from his waist. "Where's the car?" he says. "I said noon! It's noon! Where's the car?"

He doesn't look like Tom Cruise. He's a lot smaller than Tom Cruise. Small hips, small shoulders, just plain little. I wonder how they make him look so big in the movies. I wonder why these movie people have lightened his hair and also permed it. It doesn't look good. It looks overdone, exhausted, as if to shout, "Just leave me alone already!"—a sentiment very much in keeping with the mood here today.

The Daytona International Speedway is the setting for much of *Days of Thunder*, a movie that is intended to take us into the mind of Cole Trickle, a champion race car driver. The movie was entirely Cruise's idea. He is perfect for the role, number one because of his interest in car racing—he's been driving on major tracks since 1987—and number two because he's awfully good at playing the role of champion: champion teenage pimp (*Risky Business*), champion F-14 fighter pilot (*Top Gun*), champion nine-ball player (*The Color of Money*), champion bartender (*Cocktail*), champion Vietnam vet (*Born on the Fourth of July*) and so on. Something about this young man exudes the spirit of human triumph.

The car arrives. Tom puts his helmet on. "Who's going around?" he asks.

"I am," I say, stepping forward.

He looks at me, as if to size me up. "I'll go slow if you want," he says.

"No," I say. "Show me what you can do." It seems like a race carish thing to say.

And so we get strapped into a souped-up, stripped-down white Chevrolet Monte Carlo, communication wires are plugged into our helmets, and when Cruise revs the engine, the noise is so enormous, so brave, so powerful, it seems to chase all the clouds from the sky. Tom shows me what he can do.

"Do you have to drive so close to that wall?" I say.

"WHAT?" he says.

Dwarfed by this powerful machine, he is holding the steering wheel tight with both hands, moving it back and forth, like a kid pretending to drive. He's going well over 130 mph, and as he moves into the turn he pulls just inches away from a concrete wall, which is just inches away from my shoulder, which is just inches away from our sweet death.

"THE WALL!" I say. "THE WALL!"

"WHAT?" he says.

"DO YOU HAVE TO GO SO CLOSE TO WALL?"

"WHAT?" he says.

"WHAT?" I say.

It goes on like this. He throws one hand in the air as if to say, "Forget it, we won't have verbal communication," and soon we are going over 140, 150 mph. The feeling is, we are going to fly soon. And as we move around the turns, I start to see the horizon tilt, not a lot, just enough to make me queasy. I see the wall and the cloudless sky and a big white duck sitting in the middle of the oval, oblivious. We whiz by the people gathered back at the pit and then by rest rooms in a big concrete structure with a bright blue sign shouting: WOMEN. I see the images flash by, and I feel ready to fly, and I feel sick to my stomach, and I hope this movie star knows what he is doing.

"OK, COME BACK, TOM," says a voice on the radio.

He looks at me. I put my index finger up, suggesting we go around again, hoping to appear brave. In truth, I'm worried about throwing up. It wouldn't be good to throw up on Tom Cruise. This would win no points with the dragon ladies. Cruise likes the dare and heads one more time around the track.

"ALL RIGHT, TOM, COME BACK!"

I put my index finger up again. I'm trying to prove something to him, and he's trying to prove something to me. He answers me with a thumbs-up motion, and at that point we're gone, we-are-gone. He accelerates. He shows me what he can *really* do, 160, 170, 180. He goes around and around.

"TOM, COME BACK! COME BACK!"

No way, he's not about to stop. He's zooming. He's on fast forward, as if to shout, "Let go of me!" to the world. It's good to see that Hollywood has not stolen the spirit from this young man, just 27, a coveted piece of public property. We're going around and around and around. I see the wall, the sky, the duck, the people. WOMEN, wall, sky, duck, people.

"COME BACK, TOM!"

But he is deep into this flickering circle, and from my seat I get a glimpse of what it is to be Tom Cruise, whizzing through life at a superhuman pace—wall sky duck people WOMEN—defying some nagging voice.

Tom Cruise is dyslexic. Journalists sometimes refer to him as a "bad interview." They say he doesn't have a good command of the language, and so he doesn't express himself well. (The dragon ladies told me they're uneasy about him doing TV interviews because of this.)

I'm looking for it, but I don't find it. We are alone in a Holiday Inn, where I have been granted interview privileges. I don't think he is a "bad interview." I think maybe nobody's listening to this guy. He has a lot to say, and he says it slowly, deliberately, as if he's pulling each thought out, yanking it. He seems idealistic, joyful, optimistic, very American. He wants to tell me what made this country great: dedication, professionalism, integrity. Work. Work. Work. The goal is to be the best. Don't be mediocre! You don't have to be mediocre! These are his messages. Listening to Tom Cruise is like listening to Youth.

I'm here to ask him about this race car passion. Why racing? Why go around and around in a circle as fast as possible? "Racing," says Cruise, "puts you right there, at that question, you know? You can do everything perfect and just lose because your tire blows in the last lap. So it puts you right there," he says, "right at that immediate question."

"What question?" I ask.

"It's, you know, the immediacy of, Am I good? Or am I lucky?"

That question. "How do I know?" he says. "When will I know, am I good or am I lucky?"

The question is not a surprising one for someone like Tom Cruise to sit around pondering. Here is a man who was propelled to stardom so fast he barely got a chance to grow up. There he was, at 17, trying out for the high school play because his knee hurt too badly to wrestle. Just one year later he was cast in a major motion picture, *Taps*. Three years after that he zoomed to teen idol status in *Risky Business*, and then he was off co-starring with the legends: first Paul Newman, then Dustin Hoffman. Now here he is about to appear in *Days of Thunder* and billed not below but this time above another legend, the accomplished Robert Duvall.

How did he get here? People say he's intense, focused— driven, so to speak. Within the business, Cruise is known as an actor obsessed with learning his role, researching it, living it in the real world before attempting to portray it on film. Says *Days of Thunder* producer Jerry Bruckheimer, "He commits himself to being the best he can possibly be. He's got, like, blinders on." Bruckheimer's partner Don Simpson calls Cruise "Laser Head."

It's a morally superior position, people think, this idea of being driven to be the best. Especially in America. The myth is that good people are driven, and bad people are lazy, and mediocre people are just swimming in the middle somewhere. As if it's all a matter of choice.

Says Cruise: "It's not something that I consciously say, you know, 'I want to be driven.' Whatever I do, whatever I pick up, I get fascinated by it, and I want to understand it, and I get obsessed."

He tells me that driving a race car brings together many of the questions he has about his own life. And the people involved in racing, they are so much like him. "Simple and yet very sophisticated," he says. "Um, you know, you don't need an engineering degree to understand the engine. These guys just love machinery. And what you find is a tremendous dedication to what they do. Tremendous. I'm fascinated by that, by people who are absolutely obsessed with what they do."

He gets excited. "I mean, you know, people say, 'Look at the level of apathy in this country!' Well, I don't know, all's I know is for myself, when I'm learning something, there's a forward momentum. Every morning it's like you're thinking, you're on, like a train going, you're moving forward! Well, if you didn't have it, if you didn't have learning, it's like the train is stopped. Stopped! You know, stopped? And the only thing you can see is out this one little window."

The image is, he admits, a description of his own education. He was labeled the class dummy. People weren't quick to diagnose dyslexia back then. People just thought, Why can't these stupid kids read? "Oh, yeah," says Cruise. "The frustration. That frustration. Because I knew it was a failing, and I, you know, now when I talk to kids, they'll say, 'Well, you know, the educational system sucks, and you know, my teacher is so awful. . . .' And I'll say to them, 'So why depend on the system? Why sit there and expect people to hand-feed you when you can go out and get it yourself? I did. No one came up to me and said, 'Come on, I'll take you for a ride.'"

No one did, so he decided to drive himself right off the exit ramp of a miserable adolescence. Not only was he dyslexic, but his family moved a lot—his father, an electrical engineer, was constantly changing jobs. And so Cruise went to a dozen schools before he was 12 and then to four different high schools. He never had the chance to make many close friends. Plus, his parents divorced before he was a teenager. For years he lost touch with his father, who died of cancer in 1984, never having seen any of his son's films.

Cruise lived with his mother and three sisters until he was 18. He didn't even go to his high school graduation. He finished playing the lead role in his high school play and took off, having finally discovered something he was good at: acting. He moved to New York.

And now here he is, less than ten years later, a star. He wonders if it's all real. He wonders: Am I good, or am I lucky? Maybe this is how a man gets so driven. Maybe it's by trying to prove you're not driven. Maybe it's by trying to prove that you are, in fact, driving.

Says Cruise: "What is life, you know, that question: Do we create our own existence, or is it just fate?" He looks at me, as if expecting an answer, chewing on a piece of gum, working it hard.

I don't answer. We just look at each other. We're on a spiritual quest, here in this Holiday Inn. I don't know how we ended up here. The dragon ladies set this meeting up. They told me not to ask Tom about his divorce—as if this were the only interesting thing about the young man's life. I don't ask. I ask him if this obsession he has for being the best is all a matter of getting back at those people in high school who called him stupid.

"You know, that's a very small idea," he says. "That's too narrow a stake. The bigger one is: What can I do for myself, what I can do for the world, what can I do to make myself better, what do-I-want-to-do? That's what's important. Not complaining. It's done, it's over. Now it's time to flourish and prosper. People can complain about things and there's always things to complain about, but the joy in life is solving problems. You know, I remember thinking when I was growing up, I was like, 'Oh, I won't have any problems when I grow up.' And I used to fight these problems, oh, these terrible problems, and all of a sudden I realized, 'Hold it! I love problems!'

"That's what I look at. That's what I think about. You work like hell and you solve problems. You know, that's what made this country great, that-is-what-made-this-country-great! I mean, look at this country; it's built on democracy by these renegade rebels. I mean: Who the hell thought? Look at this now! Look at this! Look! That's what's important, that, you know, it's time to flourish and prosper."

And somehow the automobile, says Cruise, embodies this spirit of flourishing, prospering. "There's something about American history. When I was growing up, the automobile was a representation of the successful American. You know, the pride of America."

He says race cars always fascinated him, but it wasn't until he became friends with Paul Newman, a veteran sports car racer with whom Cruise costarred in *The Color of Money*, that he got really hooked. Newman would take Cruise racing. Their relationship grew close. "And we'd get out there on the track, and, you know, Newman would give me the sensation of being in a crowd, and bump me from behind, and come banging on the side, you know? Sensational. Sensational. I loved it."

Cruise talks about Newman as a mentor, almost as a father. Perhaps Newman in some way took the place of Cruise's dad, who was absent for so long, and the racing thing, the whole car thing, is about being with his dad. I ask him if Newman is kind of a father figure to him.

"Yeah. I mean, how can you work with Newman and not idolize him, you know, a young actor. But, wait, father figure.

That's, what do you mean by father figure? I mean, I don't like that, father figure. That's kind of a psych term, isn't it? Father figure, kind of . . . no, I don't like it.

"I never wanted to be someone else. I want to find myself and be myself. And don't get me wrong, it's no disrespect against Newman, but, I mean, I don't want to be someone else."

The phone rings. It's the dragon ladies, looking for Tom. "It's for you," I say. Our time is, apparently, up. It seems the dragon ladies have got this whole thing plotted out, how Tom Cruise shall be presented to the public, in which magazines he will appear, and on which TV shows—in which lane he'll need to drive if he wants to last. The goal isn't to finish first. The goal is to last. The goal is to become a legend—a Newman, a Hoffman, a Duvall.

He is polite. "Um, I'm still talking," he says, but they are not having it.

"COME BACK, TOM. COME BACK!" It must be such a nagging voice.

"So how about it?" I say to him, finally. "What is the answer? Are you good? Or are you lucky?"

He chews on his gum, works it. "We'll find out, won't we?"

Geraldo | 14

In Geraldo's house, there are two little finches in a cage, one named "Phil," the other "Oprah." In this house there is a lot of humor, a feeling of peace and good cheer. Geraldo says he's happy. He walks around in white shorts, no shirt, and he whistles. "What becomes of the brokenhearted." "Just call me angel." He says he's happier now than he's ever been in his life, and he says the reason is C.C. Dyer, his wife (number four). She changed him. He's not a boy anymore. He's a man.

"Are you coming?" he asks, sounding impatient. He's rather short with me, clipped, definitely not in a hospitable mood. He's touring me around the property and I'm following, but no matter how fast I walk I can't seem to keep up.

Geraldo's home is about an hour south of New York City, on the banks of the Navesink River which snakes obliviously past the lifestyles of the rich and famous. Cher lives up river, Geraldo tells me, as does Jon Bon Jovi and Bruce Springsteen. Geraldo shows me his big dogs, his macaw, his speed boat, his sail boat, his two Wave Runners, his three Jaguars, and his swimming pool surrounded by beautiful gardens with big fake rocks in them that are actually stereo speakers. He's walking fast, and I'm doing little skips.

"Come on, babe," he says. We enter the house, an enormous place, airy, with ceilings so high everyone inside looks short. Geraldo's study has no awards or pictures of Geraldo or anything like that—just a collection of big, mean knives from around the world. He takes me into his bedroom next, a sweet and cozy place with pretty floral prints. The bedroom opens to a bathroom big enough, it appears, to house a family of four.

Geraldo and C.C. moved into this house about a year ago. They were married four years ago, and have been together for about ten. At 34, she's worked as one of his producers since the days when he was a senior producer and reporter at ABC's *20/20*. In 1985, he was fired, spun into a depression and emerged—in his own opinion—a changed man. He's 47 now, wears half-moon glasses and has a perfect body.

"C.C.'s gonna be home soon," he says, as if to announce the star of this show. We've settled on the porch. Geraldo is showing me his tattoo on his right biceps: "C.C." He had it done to commemorate their first wedding anniversary. He says he won't fool around on C.C. the way he did with his other wives. He says he'll do anything to hang on to her. He's speaking softly out here on the wraparound porch with his dog, Spike, at his feet.

C.C. arrives.

"Hello, honey!" she says to Geraldo. "Oooh, hello, my Romeo! Roo-mee-ooh!" she says to the macaw. "Spikey-doodle, it's Mamma! Yeah, Mamma loves the Spikey-doodle!" she says to the dog. She screams her way through the house, greeting her pets with joy. She is wild about these pets. She is wild about Geraldo. She is wild. She has bright red hair (Geraldo and C.C. don't have to dress up for Halloween—they usually just go as Lucy and Ricky Ricardo), a lot of freckles, and the kind of energy that can be at once delightful and exhausting.

"Honey, you wanna go for a swimmy-poo?" she asks Geraldo.

He says okay. Soon some friends arrive and everyone plays in the pool. There is much laughter, but Geraldo is not the life of the party. He lies on a raft while the others splash and dive, swimmy-pooing the day away. Geraldo gets out of the pool, goes behind a bush and showers there. "Take a walk on the wild side," are the lyrics coming through the fake rock speakers. Geraldo wraps himself in a pink towel.

You'd think something dramatic or scandalous would go on at the home of the man they call "The King of Trash TV." But it doesn't. The friends leave. Geraldo and C.C. talk about having a baby. They talk about what a messy bird Romeo turned out to be. Nobody feels like cooking. We go out for dinner. Geraldo drives the mint-green '54 Jaguar, which they call "Miss Daisy," since it looks like the car in the movie. He putters slowly through the wooded streets, looking like an old man. We eat, marvel at the kiwi pancakes and after dinner Geraldo showers the chef with compliments. We drive back, saying little. "Nice night." "Yeah." Everybody is in bed by 10:30. And that's it.

In the morning, C.C. serves coffee on the porch. Geraldo has on even skimpier shorts today, a faded denim jacket and glasses. He reads *The New York Times*, and on each foot his big toe is folded up and over the other toes like he's tense. He says nothing to me, doesn't even look at me. Finally, we begin talking, this time about "The Old Geraldo."

He talks about what it was like to grow up an Hispanic Jew. He talks about having asthma as a kid. "But I forced myself to play all the sports—even though it was torture." He talks about being the underdog, being always a "minority." Hispanic, Jewish, asthmatic. Triple reason to prove himself to other guys.

Such was the birth of "The Old Geraldo." A macho, macho man. He grew up, became a lawyer, worked in the ghetto and in the 1960s fashioned himself into a working-class hero. Then he joined the staff of New York City's local Eyewitness News and became an ace investigative reporter, digging up scandals.

Meantime there were the women. He once told a *Playboy* reporter that he slept with more than 1,000 women. He imagined himself a conquistador, at work and at play.

He says he's not like that anymore. But nobody will notice. Nobody will see "The New Geraldo" for what he is. He says he's frustrated.

"There's not a day that goes by that there's not some reference to me," he says, "either as a punch line in a joke, or some allusion to the show, every single day. There's not a Sunday that goes by that I'm not in one of the comics.

"It makes me want to shake someone," he says, "and say to them, 'You don't know the trouble I've seen, you don't know how hard I've worked!'" He thinks people make fun of him because they think that he "in some way shortcut or gypped my way to the top."

I suggest that the reason people poke fun at him has to do with his style and the content of his syndicated talk show. *Geraldo!* is seen by about nine million Americans every day. I tell him about the week I watched: Geraldo hosted a program about women whose sons have been executed, another about crack babies, and another about a lady who sat up there crying because the plastic surgeon who said he would beautify her actually mangled her face and now she looked like a monster.

"Look," he says. "Today Donahue is doing a show about women who sleep with their divorced husbands. And no one will make a reference to that. Right now, I'd like you to recognize the fact that I'm probably the most serious daytime talk show in existence, in terms of topic selection."

But no one will notice. And he is frustrated.

He says a talk show host is a talk show host. And that's what he is now. But he's other things, too. He wants the world to recognize this fact: He's a serious thinker with a good heart. He's not just some showman. He's a cowboy, a pirate, a fireman, a good-guy crusader with an eye for the sensational.

He says he misses the old days as an investigative reporter when he got to be out there on the streets, digging up scandal. Now, as a talk show host, he says he walks around with a lot of pent up energy inside him. "I'm like the Hulk," he says, "ready to burst out." He stands up.

"Let's go," he says. It's late. He's got to get into the studio. He leads me down to the dock, hands me a yellow rain slicker. He says this is the thing he likes best about living in this house on a river. He gets to drive his speedboat "Bubba" to work.

He tosses his briefcase into the boat, takes one last slurp of coffee. He shows me how to sit, how to hold on, how to bend my legs and "ride it like a horse." I'm thinking this is a lot of instruction for a simple little commute to work, and then we're off, zooming down the river and entering the ocean.

There are oil tankers out here—enormous monsters of the sea—but no other boats like ours. This is just not something people do. This is like riding a bicycle down the New Jersey Turnpike.

There are, of course, waves out here. Big waves. And a storm is approaching, and this boat is moving at about 65 mph, *thawump, thawump*, through the waves, on top of them, and Geraldo, he's not saying anything, he's just concentrating on the waves, steering us into them, and the wind is whipping, and my eyes are bugged out about as far as they can go, *thawump, thawump,* this is ridiculous! I am about to be tossed into the drink. "Ride it, ride it like a horse." I'm concentrating. I'm gripping the metal bars with all my might. I'm working on my sea legs. I'm thinking about all the men and women in rush-hour traffic right now, the folks who took Amtrak, now sitting sipping coffee, reading their newspapers, living lives of comfort.

But not Geraldo. He's out here defying death. These waves are the perfect metaphor for life as he knows it. It's all a matter of conquest, of not letting the bad guys overpower you or swallow you, *thawump, thawump,* you ride on top of them, crash through them—*Yeeeee Hah!*—this is a rush.

It's how he lives. He fought his way to the top and nobody's going to take this ride away from him. He's earned it. He's proud of it. "I'm a self-made person," he tells me. "I believe fiercely in the American dream, and the ability of people to better their situation. I don't believe that ambition is a bad word. I'm basically a good person, conscientious, hard-working, you know. I worked hard. I did, I did, but that's—you know—that's enough."

A limo meets us at the dock. Geraldo has to pick out new office furniture. "What do you think of this, babe?" he asks me, as we go from store to store, and he's walking faster than ever and I'm losing my breath. Finally, I give up. So we share the rest of our time together this way, him a half block ahead, winning some race I never agreed to run.

Our
Barbies,
Our
Selves

15

In my dining room, next to a spider plant, there sits a Barbie doll. This doll was a recent gift from a friend who hoped to stitch up a certain hole in the fabric of my childhood: I grew up without ever owning a Barbie doll. Barbie was not allowed in our house. My mother said Barbie's breasts were too big.

"Huh?"

I don't remember ever discussing the issue with my mother, but I do remember wondering a lot.

Barbie, like me, is turning 30. It's weird to be the same age as Barbie. Weird to be around her after all these years. Barbie was introduced to the public on March 9, 1959, at the Toy Fair in New York, and that she has survived as America's favorite fashion doll all these years is a topic the media are having some fun with nowadays. Women columnists like to write about her. Feminists go crazy. This buxom blonde with the tiny waist, the amazing legs, the arched feet frozen for all time in the high-heel position, this plastic piece of sexism whose only interest seems to be in possessions, appearance, clothes. How can we permit such a role model for the children of the 1980s? This is what the serious-minded feminists are thinking, while I sit here, at 30, with my very first Barbie doll, thinking something different.

It is, I think, the forbidden toys that have the most profound influence.

The toys that made you wonder, wonder, wonder, all those years, the toys you saw your friends playing with but didn't dare touch, the toys that became symbols and sent you spiraling into fantastic stories, dreams, nightmares, as you are so good at doing, at 12. . . .

At 12, I'm riding my bike down the big hill that is our street, and I'm with Albert and Glen, my best friends. We're pedaling fast, faster, bringing our arms up into the air, screaming for joy in the wind. The fierce wind. It is blowing my loose t-shirt close to me, conforming to me, exposing me. What's this? I look down. Good Lord! Breasts! I'm getting breasts! I am hoping, praying Albert and Glen won't notice, that the wind will please stop, please let me go. Breasts! I can't stand this! I jump off my bike, tumble into the sky. Breasts! Maybe they will get too big, like Barbie's. Maybe I am turning into a Barbie doll. Maybe my mother won't let me in the house anymore.

"Huh?"

I have long since concluded that if mothers ever realized the full power of children's imaginations, they would never open their mouths.

Albert and Glen look back. Splat. I land on the hot asphalt, lie there, breathing hard. "What happened to her?"

Breasts.

Barbie has had a profound influence on a lot of lives, I

suspect. It says here in a press release I got from Mattel Toys that if you put all the Barbie dolls that have been sold worldwide—500 million Barbie dolls—head to toe, you would circle the world three and a half times. Well, no one has ever actually tried this, I don't think.

Confronting Barbie. There comes a time in the life of every developing female, I think, when she will inevitably confront Barbie. I pick mine up. I look at her. She is 30. I am 30. We should feel some kind of kinship, I think. Holding her now, after those long years of separation, I think Barbie and I are supposed to feel some warm glow of oneness.

"Hello, Barbie," I say.

But Barbie says nothing.

I notice that Barbie's face has changed a lot over the years. No longer does she have those bedroom eyes, encircled with ferocious eyeliner. No longer does Barbie wear that "just-shut-up-and-kiss-me-daahling" expression. Now she's perky. Her eyes are round. Her eyes say, "Jeepers, Ken, you're swell!" Mattel made the image change in the mid-1970s; presumably, the old Barbie was a bit too hot for a guy like Ken to handle. A guy like Ken. . . .

"Barbie," I say, "do you really like that dweeb?"

But Barbie says nothing to me.

I see I'm getting nowhere. What am I supposed to do with this thing? I don't know how to play Barbies. This is, of course, my mother's fault. I feel shy. Curious. Finally, I just break down and do it. I look at Barbie's breasts.

"Well, they're not that big," I say to her.

But Barbie just looks at me. It seems Barbie and I have nothing to say to one another. I shake her a bit, turn her upside down, look, wonder, hope, but in the end find in myself no warm glow, no bond of sisterhood with Barbie, no vacant spot in my heart filled up.

Instead, I am overcome by an urge to pull Barbie's head off. This is not good, I know. . . .

Shopping. Now there's a female bonding experience. I decide to take my Barbie shopping, wondering why I didn't think of this earlier. The Barbie I got is called "Fun to Dress Barbie," which means she arrived in nothing but underwear. My Barbie needs clothes. What size is she? I put a tape around her. She is 5 1/2–3 1/2–5. Hmmm. I take out my calculator. Now if Barbie were model height—let's say 5-foot-9—her measurements would be 32–20–29. Hmmm. You read it here first—scientific proof that Barbie is anatomically weird.

Anyway, I put her in my purse and take her to the store. I speak the truth when I say that both sides of aisle 10D in the Toys R Us in the neighborhood near me are lined with Barbie and her friends—Ken, Skipper, Whitney—wrapped in plastic, all of them having fun. Varying degrees of fun, it seems, most of it the kind of fun you imagine having in California, the kind of fun that can make a person miserable about life on the East Coast, in winter. Why don't I have fun like this? Why am I not living like "Island Fun Barbie," with a "wheel-popping" all-terrain vehicle, or like "Style Magic Barbie," whose skirt, the box says, doubles as a ponytail holder, or like "Beach Blast Barbie," with the "hot new wave catchin' look?"

I am beginning to get remorseful, like maybe I've just been deluding myself, thinking I have a fine life. My life is nothing compared to Barbie's. A man on a ladder is doing inventory on the Skippers. "Whew," he says to me. "A lot of Skippers." A little girl in a fur coat comes by, with her grandmother, and the two of them discuss which would be the best Barbie to buy next. I overhear the girl saying she owns 11 Barbies. Eleven Barbies! Imagine that. Enough Barbies, if you lined them up head to toe, to stretch clear across my kitchen table. Well, I've never actually tried this. The girl chooses a "California Dream Barbie," since it comes with a Beach Boys record written just for Barbie.

I get to feeling so miserable I have to get out of there, so I leave without buying Barbie anything. You know, the Beach Boys never wrote a song for me. And how come Barbie doesn't have to worry about car payments? Home insurance premiums? The IRS? Skin cancer from all that sun? How come Barbie has so much fun all the time? How come you never see Manic-Depressive Barbie? Or Barbie PMS? Or Spiritual Crisis Barbie? Or even Itchy Nose Scratchy Throat Barbie?

Where are all those Barbies? That's what I want to know, as I sit here with my Barbie doll still in her underwear. I wrap a potholder around her. Meatball Sandwich Barbie. Why not?

What you see developing here is an attitude problem. About Barbies. This is, of course, my mother's fault. You could blame your whole life on your mother.

As an important aside, I should note that I never particularly wanted a Barbie doll, as a kid; I didn't sit in my room pouting, longing for what could not be. When I would find myself around a group of girls playing Barbie, I would feel peer pressure, but I would never actually touch the Barbies. I would find other ways to participate. Once, I dug a swimming pool in my neighbor's garden, for all the neighborhood Barbies to swim in, and I even took the opportunity to learn how to pour cement. A big lump of it. Plop. It hardened. My neighbor's dad could not lift it with a shovel, and I remember he yelled a lot.

Now I am trying to open my mind, trying to be reasonable, trying to confront Barbie woman-to-woman. She's more than just a pretty face. Mattel addressed that issue a long time ago. In 1961,

Barbie joined the workforce and got a job as an airline stewardess. Her career really took off then—in the span of four years, Barbie went on to become a registered nurse, a skin diver, a fashion editor and an astronaut. Yeah, but what has she done lately? Last year, Barbie graduated from medical school and launched a fine practice, plus she came out with her own perfume, plus she got a band together and became a rock star. "Barbie and the Sensations—the all-new hip '80s group with the cool '50s look."

Interestingly, children are unimpressed by Barbie's power resume. The image of Barbie that children love most has nothing to do with Barbie's new solid position in the work force. What do girls love most? What has sold more than any other Barbie fashion in all of Barbie's 30 years?

The Barbie wedding gown.

Year after year, girls buy wedding gowns for Barbie. That's 30 years of wedding gowns. Imagine all those wedding gowns. Then multiply those by 500 million Barbie dolls, and that's enough wedding gowns, if you lined them all up head to toe, to reach from here to Saturn. Well, you could try this yourself if you don't believe me.

The Barbie wedding gown. This again brings up the question of Ken, whom Barbie first started getting married to in 1961, when she was just two years old. What is the matter with Ken? What is the matter with Ken's hair? Why is it so hard? Why doesn't it move? I see here in a book called *The World of Barbie Dolls* that in 1973 Ken decided to do something about this. He became "Mod Hair Ken," and I see here he has a bushy thing on top of his head which is puffed out, extending well beyond his shoulders. In 1974, he went back to the hardheaded look. Ken has had a lot of identity problems over the years, I think. I can't imagine it's easy for a guy. Look at Barbie. She has these breasts. Barbie is anatomically interesting. Now look at Ken. Ken has . . . nothing. Nothing. I think Ken needs a lot of hours of therapy and that Barbie should stop marrying him all the time.

Barbie has enough to do. Barbie was enclosed in the sealed bicentennial time capsule to be reopened at the tricentennial celebration in the year 2076. Barbie's popularity is a bona fide phenomenon, and I guess herein lies the root of my attitude problem. I guess I just don't get it. I read that 90 percent of little girls between the ages of four and ten in the United States today own Barbie dolls. There are black Barbie dolls, hispanic Barbie dolls, and Barbie dolls available in almost any race, creed, color or national origin. Barbie is a citizen of nearly every country in Western Europe, plus the Middle East, Australia, Latin America and the Far East. (There are no Kens in India, I'm told. What rational parent would arrange a marriage to Ken, after all?) I think it's amazing. I think it's ridiculous. I think I'll call the operator in Palo Alto, California, and ask for The Barbie Hall of Fame.

"You mean, Barbie?" the operator says to me. "Like in Barbie doll?"

"Yeah."

"You mean there's a hall of fame?" the operator says. It is a male operator. "For Barbies?"

"Yeah."

"Oh, man. . . ."

Evelyn Burkhalter owns the Barbie Hall of Fame, and she tells me her collection is 98 percent complete. Burkhalter has in her collection, under glass, nearly every doll, every article of clothing, every purse, shoe, and hot dog stand ever put out for Barbies. She tells me the museum is quite popular. She tells me the world of Barbies is bigger than I can ever imagine. "So many lives are filled with just a little bit of Barbie," she says. Every year, collectors come together for a Barbie convention, and this year's, slated for July in Los Angeles, has been sold out for months.

An original 1959 Barbie doll costs about $1,750. Brunettes are the most expensive. Blondes, I read in the *Wall Street Journal,* are slightly cheaper.

"Basically, Barbie is a magical word for something happy," Evelyn Burkhalter tells me. "She's Cinderella that stayed Cinderella. She's an amazing little person."

What has been her most dramatic change over the years? "In the new market they buy tons of Barbies," Burkhalter says, indicating that Barbie hasn't changed much at all; kids have. Kids like the one I saw in the Toys R Us with the 11 Barbies. "In the old days, kids had one Barbie. Plus possibly a Ken." Today, they have 11 Barbies, or 15 Barbies, or 20. All prepackaged with a different image. "It's weird," says Burkhalter. "It's the way she's marketed now. It's the way the world is now. There's no stability. No feeling that one thing can encompass many things."

In the end, it always comes back to your mother, your poor mother. I call her up. I bring up the subject of Barbies. I say, "Look, Ma." I tell her I'm going to write a story about how she wouldn't let me play with Barbies, and I'm going to have it published in Philadelphia, where all her friends will see.

"Oh, brother."

I'm ready for her to confess now, ready for her to say how wrong she was on this Barbie issue, but when I see the conversation is not going my way, I just sit back and listen. "Of course you can see I was right now, can't you?" she says. "Can't you? I just did not want this fashion doll to be a role model for my children." I don't remember it being presented this way before. All I remember hearing is "breasts." "Breasts too big."

The Barbie issue for me was an issue of sexuality. The message I got was this: You are a person first, a woman second—as if being female were an extra thing, an afterthought, an embarrassment. Naughty and forbidden like Barbie. The issue was of being broken up into two, or three, or four or more—feeling confused, feeling shattered. The issue is, after all, the issue of the forming adult. Coming to realize that "one thing can encompass many things." Discovery of self is the act of uniting many selves, I think.

On the one hand, my mother was quite progressive; she did a wonderful thing at a time when it wasn't popular like it is now. She instilled in us a belief that women are more than the sum of their biological parts. Women have minds. Women have souls. Women have creative selves waiting inside to be unleashed. She believed this. And I believe this. And I believe that women have many other selves, too, that women have sexual selves, that every woman is Barbie, somewhere inside her, and rather than deny her, rather than kick her out of the house, why not claim her, celebrate her, invite her over for dinner, invite her to be a part of the party that is the whole of you?

Not that I reach this peaceful conclusion without a bit of torment. If truth be told, I did pull my new Barbie's head off one day. Plink! It was easy. Inside, it said, "Mattel Inc. 1976," which means her head is ten years younger than her torso, which says, "Mattel, Inc. 1966 CHINA." Anyway, I put her head back on and now she looks better, although I guess I messed something up because now her head sort of dangles. You know, she's always leaning over now, sitting here in my dining room wearing a potholder—some women look good in anything—her head is perpetually cocked, like she's always wondering, always saying, "Huh?"

A Garden in Winter   16

This was supposed to be the weekend I put my garden to bed for winter—time to clip the lilac suckers, mulch some perennials, and tuck in a few last bulbs—but instead I'm on train to Philadelphia to say goodbye to a friend who is dying. I had planned for my hands to be happily immersed in dirt, but then I got the call asking, "Will you come hold my hand?" She never asked me to hold her hand before. I'm thinking about her, and my garden, and suddenly I'm reconfirming my resolve to specialize in perennials, plants that only pretend to die. They surprise you each spring with a resurrection you never really believe in, but then there it is.

Some gardeners here in Zone 6 are engaged right now in the noble struggle to make winter gardens grow. I hear tales of plastic sheeting over spindly carrot plants and other extravagant ways to deny frost. Year-round gardening is possible, depending on what kind of gardener you are and what you're in it for. People grow spinach, lettuce, beets and cabbage all winter long. And leeks, you can always count on leeks. To get these crops to grow you have to fuss with the aforementioned sheets of plastic, and bales of straw, and corrugated cardboard, and drip irrigation watering systems, and all manner of complicated doohickeys one concocts to beat winter at its own game.

I am not one of these gardeners. For one thing, I don't grow vegetables, only flowers. Secondly, I enjoy the change of seasons too much to want to tussle with them and try to make them behave my way. Generally speaking, I have always found that it is more fun to ride the winds of change than it is to do battle with them. And anyway, I believe that the most delightful winter garden is the one you have in your head.

Winter is a time for thinking, planning, imagining how beautiful your yard will be next year, even though this year it may not have turned out so good. Winter is a gardener's holiest time, an opportunity to examine the stupid sins of last year's growing season, and repent. Only in winter do you have time to read all those garden books you acquired with such lust over the summer. You can focus on the details of what any given plant was supposed to do, according to the books, and compare that information to your plant's less than exemplary life story. You try to store growing hints in your brain until next year so you'll be a better gardener, a smarter gardener, the greatest gardener in the world, perhaps, but usually you don't, and so you aren't, and deep down you know you never will be. Winter is a time to stare out the window at your barren plot and wonder why in the world you bother.

How did this garden become so important?

The window I'm looking out right now displays not my garden but a pumpkin patch whizzing by. The people sitting behind me on the train are talking about the old lady who fell off the train last year. She wasn't paying attention as she walked from car to car, to car to car, all the way to the back of the train, to the last car, to the last door, out of which she stepped and landed—

plop—on the railroad bed. They didn't find her for two days. She didn't die, though. The people behind me are saying she must have been a crazy lady, or else drunk. I don't know why they aren't blaming the train, instead of the lady.

The lady I am going to visit is crazy, some people say. This makes me mad. She's hard to get along with, I guess, and can get ornery. She is 87 years old and fully in charge of her life. People call her "The Balloon Lady" because she flies balloons.

I've always liked visiting her because she can so quickly delight in how ridiculous and pathetic the world looks sometimes. Politicians make her laugh. Accountants make her laugh. Lawyers make her laugh. Doctors make her laugh. Corporate America makes her laugh. She laughs at all that she refuses to believe in. Maybe this is the definition of crazy; I don't know.

She lives alone. She's taken care of herself, lived an adventurous life, and even in old age refuses to be cared for. She's not seen a doctor or taken a drop of medicine in over a half century. A week ago, at home, she had a stroke. She called an ambulance. She lasted a week in the hospital before she drove the doctors crazy enough to let her go home. The stroke took away control of her mouth and right eye and her ability to walk. They put one of those automatic beds in her dining room and a portable toilet next to it. And here she was left.

She tried to sleep in that bed. By midnight the first night she had climbed out of it. She got on her hands and knees and crawled up the steps to her old bed. She called me. Here she would sleep, she said. Here she would die, she said. That was when she asked me to come hold her hand.

I came into gardening the way all true gardeners come: I took a path of utter ignorance. I knew next to nothing about plants when I bought my house and inherited this amazing yard. It's kind of an odd setup. My house sits at the end of a compact city street where there are no front yards. No yards at all, really, except mine, which runs along the side and back of my house, an "L" shaped stretch of land that separates me from a railroad track. Freight trains come moseying by a few times a day. I have come to depend on the clatter and I like waving to the conductors when I'm out there pulling weeds. Mine is an urban garden, a little oasis, a mini-paradise surrounded by the noise and smells and warmth of the city.

As I said, I knew next to nothing about gardening when I moved here. And the truth is I didn't want to know much. I just wanted some pretty colors and sweet aromas to walk among. I looked at a few garden books and, like a lot of people, I suspect, I did exactly what the garden books said not to do. "Don't just go out to the local nursery and buy a bunch of plants," they all warn, in so many words. "You have to plan your garden. You have to think in terms of color patterns, basic groupings of line and form, harmony and accord, subtle balances of scale and proportion, mass and texture."

Yeah, yeah, texture smexture, I thought. I just wanted flowers. I went to my local nursery and discovered that flowers come in basically two types: The kind you only have to plant once because they come back every year, and the kind you have to keep planting over and over again because they die every year. Now, why would I want a plant that was just going to die on me, I reasoned, and so I stayed in the perennial section of the nursery. Next I discovered that perennials come in basically two types: the kind that bloom for a long time and the kind that bloom for a short time. Now, why would I want a plant that hardly ever blooms, I reasoned, and so all my garden decisions were made. I perused the nursery and read all the little tags attached to all the little plants and if it said "blooms all summer," I bought it. The only exception to this rule was that if it was a plant I had heard of. These I also bought—

lavender, baby's breath, daisies, and other numbers on the gardening greatest hits list.

I took my garden home in my hatchback. No problem. It was as easy as buying a new set of dishes. I pulled each plant out of its pot and stuck it in the ground. I turned on the hose, looked up at the sun, said, "Go for it, guys," and felt happy. I would now have flowers, all summer long, for the rest of my life.

Well, you know the rest of the story. Some plants died immediately and some waited (politely) a few weeks before they died, and most stuff just sort of sat there and did nothing for the first year, and a few plants took over and grew so big and tall they smothered the smaller plants, and I couldn't remember what any of them were called, and I got really disgusted by all these rude bugs that came in and gnawed on my plants—"SLUGS!"—and then there were all those damn weeds—"Is that a weed, or is that a plant I want?"—that just cluttered up everything, and then it wouldn't rain enough, and then it would rain too much, and by September of the first year I was suffering from a fairly profound depression.

The heck with this, I said.

How I got from this point to my present delightful obsession with all things that grow in a garden—perennials as well as annuals and shrubs and weeds and beetles—is a mystery gardeners throughout the ages have likewise pondered, I suspect. I believe the earth continues to call you, once you get your hands in it.

A garden is a relationship. You wouldn't have started it if you knew what you were getting yourself into: something difficult and messy and maintenance intensive. Still, it fills up empty spots you never even knew you had inside you. You dig deeper and deeper into the earth and the joy you take from your time on this planet becomes richer and more complicated and fuller than that of any dimension your mind could have invented.

My relationship with my 87-year-old friend began about ten years ago. I was writing a series of stories about old ladies and she was the most intriguing of all, a balloonist who spent her life breaking world records up in the sky. Her balloons made her famous. She flew with movie stars and U.S. Presidents, and became a legend in the aviation world. She was a wildly eccentric character who loved flying—almost as much as she loved cutting the grass. Often when I'd visit she'd be just climbing down off a gigantic farm tractor, proudly displaying the grass runway she had just mowed smooth. She did this for her husband, a pilot who would land his airplane there. She did this for him years after he had died, as if expecting him to zoom out of heaven and come back in for a landing at any moment. A lot of people said she was crazy for doing that, but she didn't care, and neither did I. Often she and I would get in her car and drive down the runway, just for fun. "See how smooth it is, dear! Velvety smooth!" Other than that we would just eat lunch, talk, maybe go to the bakery, or explore the fields of wild flowers. My visits became more frequent over the years as the bond between us grew tighter, and although we loved each other, I can't say we ever got to know each other very well at all.

I feel a similar way about my flowers. I mean I don't know these things, not really. I don't understand them. I don't understand why some of them crawl into the earth in the winter and then reappear in the spring, and some of them just throw seeds and then give up living, and some of them propagate with cuttings, and some you have to break up every two years, and some just go along happily cloning themselves with underground tubers. How remarkable! I keep finding more and more plants I want to try, just to see how each has worked out this game of growing, propagating, and dying—the same game all of us are in, I guess.

My garden now is broken up into areas I think of as rooms, connected by hallways. The hallways are lined with day lilies and begonias and impatiens and easy stuff you can count on. Right outside my kitchen door is the living room. In summer I have a formal flower bed there—blue salvia, snapdragons, blankets of sweet alyssum—and lots of pots of geraniums edged with lobelia, like you see in Ireland. Up the hill and beyond the lilacs, sort of hidden away, is a big room I think of as the bedroom. It's kind of a private area, just for me, a reading space and a sipping Diet Coke space, and last year the clematis vine went wild up there and filled the place up like Eden. Next year I'm thinking: more clematis. Maybe some jackmani this time, or montana. And also: morning glory. Flowering vines definitely inspire greed in me.

Way out in the front of my yard, by the picket fence, is the playroom. This is where the largest flower beds are and the place I try out new plants just for fun. This is my favorite room because this is where most of my perennials are, or at least where most of them were born before they got transplanted to other beds. Bleeding heart, red cloud spider wort, edelweiss, columbine, bee balm, sea pink, salvia, silver mound, primrose, lavender, hosta by the ton, yarrow, lythrum, astilbe in many colors and heights—and countless others. My cat sleeps in a huge mat of coreopsis on summer's hottest days, and at night when I get home I have to comb it upward and help it stand up straight again. I'm quite bonded to that coreopsis, somehow, but then again so is my cat.

I don't really have a favorite plant. Like a good parent, I don't arrange love that way. My perennials do thrill me with their loyalty, though. I'll be snooping around in the garden in spring and there one of them will be, all supple and tender, rising from the earth, yawning after some excellent hibernation. And my heart will leap up. "Hey!" I'll say, "Hello there!" right out loud. So begins a summer-long conversation.

My mind is wandering like crazy on this train. There's an Amish boy across the aisle from me, reading a book on horse breeding. In front of him is a boy his same age with a Walkman turned to maximum volume so we can all hear the tinny beat over top the train's low rumble.

I'm thinking about that lady who fell off the train. I wonder what it would be like to fall though mid air and be left alone like that—while everybody else just keeps on going, whizzing down the tracks—and there goes your luggage and everything else. Is that the feeling of death or is that just how we fear death will be? We get dumped somewhere and watch the world chug on without us, getting smaller and smaller until it disappears, nobody even noticing we fell off.

That's the fear, I suppose, but I don't think that's what death will be like at all. I don't think we'll care at all about the train that keeps on going without us.

When plants stop blooming surely they don't miss their days of blooming, do they? Blooming is just a stage. The flower falls to the ground, returns to the earth, and becomes food for other plants. Where did we ever get the notion that the bloom was the only real thing, that everything before it and after it had to be defined in terms of it? What if the bloom, the life, were defined in terms of death. Then death would be the real thing and life would be just something you do in order to get there.

When the train finally pulls into 30th Street Station I get a taxi, and when I arrive at my friend's house, I let myself in. I see the automatic bed in the dining room that she abandoned, and the toilet. "Hello?" I yell.

"Hello, dear," she says, "Up here." I go up into her bedroom, a place I was never allowed to enter before. It is very messy and very dusty. She is lying there, in a single bed, in the darkness of the late afternoon. I put the light on. "Look at that tree," she says, motioning toward the window where a tall oak stands. "Isn't it wonderful?"

"Wonderful," I say, thinking, this is it? This is how she's been amusing herself? Not with some TV show—well, she's never owned a TV—not with her beloved Larry King whom she would never miss on the radio, not with the books that were once her passion. She just wanted to watch the oak tree.

"My feet are freezing," she says. "Would you fix the blankets?"

I go over and smooth them out around her feet and then tuck in her shoulders too.

"You're good at this," she says. "Have you been tucking in a lot of dying old ladies?"

"No, you're my first," I say. We laugh. She reaches out for my hand and I give it to her. Her skin is surprisingly soft. How do old people get baby's skin? I wonder.

"Guess what," she says, "I've decided not to die."

"That's good," I say.

"I'll die when I'm good and ready," she says.

"Would you like some soup?" I ask.

"Yes, dear," she says. "Let's have a picnic right here."

I bring up the bed tray with two bowls of soup and some bread and coffee and I'm pleased to see her appetite is so large. But she is clumsy and has trouble feeding herself. The soup spills down her front. She is wilting. I face this. Night is falling and she asks me to turn on the outside light, which just happens to throw a spot on the oak tree.

"Isn't that wonderful?" she asks.

"Wonderful," I say, adding, "You want me to bring up the radio or something? Or why don't you try and read?"

"Oh, no," she says. "I have to watch the tree."

"All right."

"What are you working on now?" she asks. "Are you writing something funny?"

"An essay about my garden in winter," I say. Something about death and resurrection, I tell her. Or something about how flowers leave you, eventually, just like friends. So why bother? Well, because that's just the way it works, that's why.

"That's nice, dear," she says. "I love you, too."

We say goodbye. It feels like years go by before I finally make it back home to my garden, the tracks, the cat, my coreopsis crackling like brittle tumbleweed in the breeze. I get on my knees and cover the coreopsis with a blanket of shredded bark. I put the few last tulip bulbs in, a stately row of them between the picket fence and a patch of grape hyacinths due up in April.

It's good to stick your hands in the dirt sometimes. You can own the smallest plot of land in America and still it would be four thousand miles deep. You start digging with your mind and pretty soon you're doing a free fall right through China. It's good to take a journey like that sometimes.